NO PLACE
BUT HERE

Garret Keizer

NO PLACE
BUT HERE

*A Teacher's Vocation
in a
Rural Community*

VIKING

VIKING
Published by the Penguin Group
Viking Penguin Inc., 40 West 23rd Street,
New York, New York 10010, U.S.A.
Penguin Books Ltd, 27 Wrights Lane,
London W8 5TZ, England
Penguin Books Australia Ltd, Ringwood,
Victoria, Australia
Penguin Books Canada Ltd, 2801 John Street,
Markham, Ontario, Canada L3R 1B4
Penguin Books (N.Z.) Ltd, 182–190 Wairau Road,
Auckland 10, New Zealand

Penguin Books Ltd, Registered Offices:
Harmondsworth, Middlesex, England

First published in 1988 by Viking Penguin Inc.
Published simultaneously in Canada
1 3 5 7 9 10 8 6 4 2

Page 165 constitutes an extension of this copyright page.

LIBRARY OF CONGRESS CATALOGING IN PUBLICATION DATA
Keizer, Garret
No place but here.
1. Keizer, Garret.   2. High school teachers—Vermont
—Biography.   3. Rural schools—Vermont.   I. Title.
LA2317.K335A3   1988   373.11′0092′4   87-40543
ISBN 0-670-81498-9

Printed in the United States of America by
Arcata Graphics, Fairfield, Pennsylvania
Set in Sabon

For Kathy, Sarah, and the Northeast Kingdom,
the names that mean home

Acknowledgments

Thanks are due to Elaine Jones for helping me prepare my manuscript; to Helen and James Hayford, Kathy Keizer, and Howard Frank Mosher for serving as readers; to Mr. Mosher again for proposing the book in the first place; to Charles Verrill, my editor, for his good advice; to the Lake Region school board for granting me a sabbatical in which to write; and to the people of my community for supporting me financially and morally during that time.

Two acknowledgments implicit in the book but worth mentioning at the start are to the students of Lake Region Union High School, who have given me my best education, and to my former supervisor, Donna Underwood. For seven years she showed me how a good teacher works, and in the year this book was written, she showed me how a brave one dies.

Contents

NO PLACE
BUT HERE

Seeking Our Welfare

But seek the welfare of the city where I have sent you into exile, and pray to the Lord on its behalf, for in its welfare, you will find your welfare.

—JEREMIAH

I never cared less about whether I lived or died than I did my first year of teaching. I never worked harder, I never learned more than I did then. I never went anywhere that was more important for me to go than to these remote counties, though I did not know that then. I thought I had come to the end of the world and to what might as well be the end of my life.

What I remember most about my ride up to interview for the job was a heap of snow on the border of a hayfield. It was late May. I had driven to northeastern Vermont before, but never in spring and never with the aim of living there. I had come once as a boy on summer vacation from New Jersey and had caught my first big trout, and had come again fishing when my wife and I lived in Burlington on Lake Champlain.

Now I was driving up with my few memories of the place, all of them pleasant, but tempered by what some Vermont friends had seen fit to tell me: that in Irasburg a gang had shot up the house of a black minister and his white woman companion, which is true; that the most popular high school graduation gift was a set of false teeth, which is not true; that if I stayed long enough I'd be "lost" somehow, which is somehow true, as well as funny and fortunate. At the time, all I knew for sure was that the Orleans Central school district needed a high school English teacher and a speech pathologist, that my wife and I seemed to fit the bill, and that if there was still snow on the ground in May, we'd better have a couple of periscopes for January.

We found an apartment in Orleans, within sight and sound of the furniture mill which makes Orleans a mill town and which made our four-hundred-mile exodus from industrial New Jersey to "rural" Vermont seem a bit like carrying coals to Newcastle. On my first morning in town I took a walk to the hardware store. Across the street in a rusty pickup truck a man who had apparently misplaced or outgrown his graduation present leaned out his window and shouted to me.

"Hey, buddy, did anybody ever tell you you were bowlegged?"

He said so, it seemed, not to insult me so much as to wake me up, as if he were calling to a driver with an unhung exhaust system and wondering just how damn long somebody could drag a thing like that around and not notice. I was wearing pants cut off at the knees.

"Are you talking to me?" I shouted back.

"Yeah, I'm talking to you. You're bowlegged as hell!"

This was a misleading introduction to the community but a proper introduction to being a teacher—it was at that moment that I felt myself become one, not because being a teacher means being insulted, but because being a first-year teacher in a small town, one does not flip somebody the bird on Main Street. In my first exercise of professional restraint, I entered the store shaking my head and bought three gallons of white latex to paint our rooms, which were yellow, pink, green, and purple. By November I would be knee-deep in snow and compositions, cursing my stupidity for having forsaken urban salaries to live behind a rural factory, and for taking a master's in English in order to take attendance in study hall, and for studying English in the first place because I wanted to write, when now I would probably never have the time or the soul to write again.

Seven years later I am still teaching, and I am writing a book about the work I once thought would keep me from writing.

More specifically, I am writing an essay on teaching in a rural community. It is that simply because a rural community is the only place in which I have taught. Rurality is my context more than my subject, though to some extent it must be both. I write my essay on teaching in a rural community not as a soldier would write about making war in a desert—where lack of water and cover define the very strategy—but as a lover might write about his affair in a village, where the mountains and verandas have determined the moods and the occasions of love, but have made the loving itself little different than it is elsewhere. At least this is what I suppose—as I say, I have taught no place but here.

It may be that I refrain from emphasizing my locale for fear of simplifying it, of exaggerating its remoteness or uniqueness, which is always the temptation when one writes of a lesser-known place, and which ought always to be suspect in an age of so few truly remote places. If El Dorado exists, it is as likely to contain a pair of golden arches as a network of golden streets. The Northeast Kingdom is no less fabulous or familiar. Moose and marijuana both make appearances on the school grounds. My students rent video machines and are mangled in baling machines. I can cite cases of child abuse as shocking as any that occur to the south, and I can cite examples of families so unreal in the degree of their wholesomeness that their portrayal in a film would guarantee its being panned as a sappy piece of mythology.

The Northeast Kingdom comprises three counties: Caledonia, Essex, and Orleans, and is bordered on the east by northern New Hampshire and on the north by Quebec. The school at which I teach is called Lake Region Union High School, and we do live in a region of glacial lakes, all cold and beautiful, and of mountains, forests, and dairy farms. There is little industry, almost nothing to mar the landscape— but little, too, of the emphatic quaintness one sometimes finds in southern Vermont. I know of no town in the area that gives the impression of having no life beyond tourist season. Sunshine is statistically and noticeably less here than in most places; poverty, more. There are relatively few of us, and at least a third of the newspaper's letters to the editor are by people one knows, or has heard about.

The variety of those people has to be one of the Northeast Kingdom's most extraordinary characteristics, and therefore a noteworthy characteristic of its public schools. We are a surprisingly diverse community. A number of our people are of French Canadian descent, a fair number of my students come from bilingual homes; now and then, a student is the first of his or her family to speak English. In the early 1970s a sizable influx of "counterculture" people migrated to the region, where cheap land, natural beauty, and proximity to the Canadian border formed an ideal setting for the founding of communes, several of which are still in existence. The professional class appears equally divided between local men and women who came home after college and sundry "flat-landers" like me. Artists, fugitives, entrepreneurs, and mes-siahs have all on occasion found the Northeast Kingdom an amenable place to settle. The remarkable thing is not that one can list so many types on a piece of paper, but that one can see so many in the same grocery store, bar, or theater, and see them not as odd fellows who happened to be shuffled together by the conditions of a mass transit system or a job market, but as neighbors who live—I can only say deliberately—in the same small place, and who think of it consciously as a place, the Northeast Kingdom, not just northeastern Vermont.

Nevertheless, despite this variety, most of my students have lived most of their lives here, many on farms. Whatever their origins, all of them are in some sense isolated, for better and for worse, by living here. That isolation has a number of effects. From a teacher's point of view the major negative ones are a lack of confidence and a lack of exposure. Obviously, the two are related.

When I interviewed for my job that afternoon I saw the heap of snow in May, a teacher said to me, "The kids here tend to think of themselves as just hicks from the sticks." To some extent they do, though most would resent that choice of words. What a reader must remember is that this self-image is as much a product of the larger culture as it is a condition of my students' particular locale. Despite some fond illusions about "life on the land," despite the bucolic settings of our soft drink commercials, the American mainstream is pitifully ignorant of and indifferent to its rural population. Our politicians can't even seem to remember that schools close in the summer not to give teachers a rest or a compensation for their low salaries, but to enable farm kids to bring in the hay.

One of those kids once asked me, with an echo of "Yeah, how come?" from her fellows, "How come on television, when there's somebody from Vermont, they always make him look dumb?" They were thinking of three idiot brothers named Larry, Darryl, and Darryl on *Newhart*. I tried to explain that their comic representatives were made to "look dumb" for much the same reason that their serious writers were made out to be "regional." Even the deprivations of some of my students would seem to lack the proper credentials. Real poverty is urban poverty. People in the city are poor because they are oppressed, discriminated against, and alienated; people in the country are poor because they're too stupid to realize they ought to be living in the city.

I think it may have been the recognition of this prejudice that gave me my first sense of common ground with my students, a sense that would grow more and more as I taught them, and that at its best would be felt as solidarity with them. For teachers are the hicks of the professional world. But that realization came later. What came first was that the only hope of salvation offered to them or to me was "getting out"—of the Northeast Kingdom and of teaching, respectively. I took both hopes seriously. Like many rural teachers, I was overly enamored of "the great big world out there," failing to realize that I was in nothing so provincial as in my subservience to that "great big world."

Nevertheless, I have mentioned my students' need for exposure alongside their need for confidence, and there is no excuse for downplaying the first need in order to lessen the second. Our students do need more exposure to what the world beyond these mountains has to offer; meeting that need has to be one of the major objectives of our teaching here. It also has to be the occasion for some of our greatest satisfactions, as when a student who has seen Boston and probably a large city for the first time says, "Now whenever I go to sleep, I think of all those people behind all those windows—people I'll never know, with their own lives—and they're going to sleep, too."

Or, when a student goes home and tells her mother, as the mother then told me, "Mr. Keizer comes into homeroom and he says, 'Would you like to hear some music?' and we don't think nothing of it, so we say, 'All right.' And what does he put on? The opera! I thought I'd die. Well, I got to listening to it there, and you know, it weren't half bad."

It occurs to me that playing a portion of "the opera" (actually a Brandenburg Concerto) for this young woman may have been the single most important thing I have done in seven years of teaching. It also occurs to me that her last four words, which I have repeated often to myself in the course of my bowlegged sojourn here, are a fitting if understated summation both of the things I still need to teach and of the time I have spent teaching. Of the latter I must say, it weren't bad at all.

A Promised Land

Mister, I ain't a boy, no, I'm a man,
And I believe in a promised land.

—Bruce Springsteen,
"The Promised Land"

When the great cathedral of Notre Dame de Chartres burned in 1194, enthusiasm for its restoration swept through France. Among those who organized for the work were troops of children and teenagers who descended on Chartres like harbingers of the apocalypse. Unfortunately, it is more accurate to speak of them as precursors of the Children's Crusade, which left for the Holy Land in 1212, and arrived instead at the slave markets of Baghdad and Cairo, thanks to two unspeakable merchants named Hugh the Iron and William the Pig.

We hear such stories and their modern parallels, and we shudder at the enormous energy and credulity of youth. We sigh our thanks for living in a better place and time, and we send the kids off to the video arcade.

But the energy remains. That its use has often been tragic does not make its waste any less tragic. That we do waste it, that we have allowed it to be perverted into a subculture of obnoxious mannerisms and indiscriminate consumerism does not make it any less marvelous to consider.

These young people need a challenge—that is one of our great clichés—but our conception of challenge has become so bland that we might as well be saying they need their vitamins or their sleep. We frequently approach the education of our youth with the implied assumption that they do not want to learn, or that they will learn only in terms of the latest movies, records, and posters, which were designed, of course, not by rebellious fifteen- and sixteen-year-olds, but by comfortable twenty- to forty-year-olds desirous of being more comfortable. We assume that the only poetry our students will read is on an album jacket, the only research they will do concerns marijuana or the major leagues, and the only novel they will study is about a prostitute with pimples. We accept their initial groans at the introduction of anything different as sincere and insurmountable, not realizing that they are only reacting as they have been taught to react by a few moronic TV sitcoms which they themselves but half enjoy.

I accept the groans as points of etiquette, and proceed. My freshman English classes read *Antigone, The Odyssey, Macbeth,* Hardy's *Return of the Native*—none of these abridged or paraphrased. I begin our study of these works by stating that I can think of several reasons why we shouldn't study them and that other persons have supplied me with several more, that I reject the reasons out of hand and that we are going to study the classics come what may. I will not pretend that the books are not difficult, and I will not pretend that they are without passages which most modern readers will find tedious—but I will also not pretend that tripe is profound or that people lack sensibility simply because they are fifteen and live "in the sticks." So we begin to read. And the response from the majority of students is one of mature commitment, unfeigned enjoyment, and surprising insight.

Of course one does not tackle *Macbeth* in remedial English. But the principle behind tackling it elsewhere remains in full force here. For several years I taught a class called Reading and Writing, which had been designed for students with difficulty in both. Halfway through one semester I announced to my "lovable thugs" that we were abandoning the worksheets and undertaking the writing of a book. The size of the class—three boys—had been something of an accident, and I realized almost too late that such an accident with all its possibilities was not likely to happen ever again. For their part, the boys sank ever lower in their seats, presumably in a quandary over whether to kill themselves or me. I went on to tell them that when the book was written we would probably have it printed and sell it to the school population and to local libraries. They were relieved: something in the teacher had obviously "snapped" and he would be committed before any of this actually happened. But we did write a book, a hot-rod picaresque called *Born to Run,* or, as I nicknamed it, "Smokey and the Bandit Meet Strunk and White"—though nothing in the Good Ol' Boy genre has moments as touching and near to sublime as *Born to Run.* We sold out in two lunch periods and got reviewed in the local paper; the authors received an award at the June assembly. Years later I still get questions about "them guys that wrote the book." Them guys have been placed among the stars.

But when they were still on earth, one of them said to me, "I told my mom what we're up to, and she said, 'You can't even spell—how the hell are you gonna write a book!'" This was just my point. If a kid can't spell, have him write a book. If a kid can't clear the low hurdles, give him a shot at the high.

That he will frequently clear the high is not so mysterious as it seems. Kids are no different from other human beings in that they want to matter. Recently the son of some dinner guests, bored by our conversation, asked if I had any work around for him to do. I told him he could throw some firewood from a smaller pile into a larger one. I could tell he did not believe that was something I really needed done, and he came back in five minutes claiming to be tired. I wound up doing the job myself that Saturday. Had I asked him to block and split ten cords of tree-length logs with a chain saw and maul, he doubtless would have worked into the dark. But he refused to be "kept busy," and I respect him for that. He wanted to engage in something purposeful. He was willing to work, but only if I was willing to take a risk.

I have sometimes said that the best way to handle the kids who pose the biggest discipline problems in a school is to put them in charge of discipline. I am only half fooling. I think a major problem in our schools is not that kids are too brash and nervy but that we are not brash and nervy enough.

Nowhere is this more apparent than in our insipid campaigns for "school spirit" and "student leadership." We vainly hope to make a treadmill look like a sacred quest; we ask kids to be excited in a void of ideas, because only in talking about nothing can we be sure not to arouse any controversy. We don't even talk to them about patriotism anymore. We ask kids to take a stand in all the places where we have been taking a nap. Then, when we have few takers, we complain about the apathy of youth.

The so-called "rebelliousness" of youth—which often appears as little more than the hard edge of apathy—may also come from our failure to issue a significant challenge to our young. In public education, as in popular entertainment, we have sold our kids a curious bill of goods on the subject of rebellion. First we tell them that rebellion is basically good, creative, liberating. The bright lights of science, art, and politics were all rebels. Second, we tell them that rebellion is the natural attitude of youth. It's healthy, inevitable, and to some extent tolerable for the young to rebel. Assuming we're right on the first two points, we ought to add a third: that rebellion is only as good, creative, and liberating as its opposition is strong, coherent, and not totally disarmed by points one and two. To quote the poet Hugh MacDiarmid, somewhat out of context: "You cannot strike a match on a crumbling wall." Take classicism away from the Romantics who rebelled against it and what does one have left? A few surly extras on the set of *Rebel Without a Cause*. Take away every claim of authority from our pronouncements, and thus any clear point of departure for a young thinker, and what does one have left by way of youthful rebellion? A few mannerisms less original than James Dean's.

An interesting observation in this regard is my students' understanding of the word "radical." The term arose in discussion one day, and it was not long before I realized that my students and I were talking about two different things. Finally I asked them what a "radical" is. As nearly as I can quote their definition, a radical is an outrageously fun-loving person. At first I was amazed at their innocence. But in retrospect I am even more amazed at how accurately they had described their own predicament—and for that matter, how accurately they had intuited the nature of so much American middle-class "radicalism." In the absence of any real challenge, given or received, when opponents assume postures more than they take stands, we're pretty much left with "fun," aren't we? If reaching or redefining a promised land is not the "radical's" business, then all that remains is to raise a little hell.

Our failure to challenge kids to purposeful leadership, or even to provoke them to creative rebellion, is matched by a still more significant failure to acquaint them with great ideas. It is not simply our school assemblies and slogans that are so bland and pointless, but the tenor of our curriculum. Kids are shockingly unaware of the religious and political ideas that have shaped their history and are even now revolutionizing their world. In a century torn by ideological struggles we seem to think that the best favor we can do for our young is to have them ignorant of all ideology. I wonder if any of them assume what their elders seem to have assumed, that the safest way to assure pluralism is to bury it in nihilism.

A bright student came to me several years ago with a question on her mind. She'd been watching a television series on the Holocaust. "What's a Jew?" she asked. "They don't believe in God, right?" As gently as I could, I explained that her phrase "believe in God" was essentially a Jewish invention, or discovery if she preferred. She acknowledged the debt with an "oh!" but then wanted to know why the Nazis were so anti-Semitic. Like many other students, she thought that the Nazis had invented anti-Semitism. And like many other students, she probably could have located Israel on a map, named its prime minister, and recited the dates of its wars and founding. She would have been able to do the same for Iran and the Soviet Union. She just could not tell me in any detail what many a Jew, Muslim, or Marxist has lived and died for.

Admittedly, we often shy away from acquainting students with ideas because we fear indoctrinating those ideas, or distorting them with a teacher's bias. That is a good fear to have. I know of a school in the Northeast Kingdom where a young girl, who may one day be an important scientist, was persecuted in a science class for her beliefs on the origins of humankind. Her ideas were quite conventional: she accepted Darwin wholeheartedly. Her teacher, if I must call him that, disagreed—and argued his case for "creationism" by repeatedly making monkey noises at the girl, an argument her less-evolved classmates found easy to copy. Apparently his understanding of ethics was as profound as his definition of *science.* Those who may seem overly zealous to prevent this kind of travesty are not such extremists after all. But the same vigilance we exercise to keep science classes from turning into Sunday school classes needs to be exercised to prevent legitimate fears from turning into superstitions. It is possible for students and teachers to explore "alien" ideologies (provided they are not utterly alien to the discipline being taught) without alienating one another.

Once a girl in my class decided to do a research paper on the John Birch Society. Her father was a Bircher, as she herself was soon to become, so this her first major research paper was a rite of passage as well. Perhaps because I was so enthusiastic over her choice of a topic, she assumed I was also sympathetic to her political point of view. Almost conspiratorially she confided to me her worries about a history teacher who would also be reading her paper and giving it a grade. "Mr. M——is a pretty liberal guy, and I'm worried how he'll mark it," she said.

I assured her that Mr. M——would insist, as I would, on an objective presentation of factual material and on sources other than publications of the Society, but that our insistence did not in any way imply a prejudice against her or her work. "As far as politics go," I told her, "mine are probably a good deal to the *left* of Mr. M——'s, and look how excited I am about your paper." I had meant to put her at ease, but my mistake was immediately evident from the blood leaving her face. From where she stood, Mr. M——looked as pink as a piece of rare prime rib, and I was to the *left* of that? Removing my glasses so as to blur even the slightest resemblance I might have to Trotsky, I smiled with great benevolence. "It's going to be a wonderful paper," I said. It's going to be the end of my life, she thought.

Well, it was a wonderful paper, and working on it with her was the beginning of one of the warmest relationships I ever enjoyed with a student. I tried not only to help her see different points of view, but also to give depth to her own. I introduced her to the novels of Ayn Rand. I found quotations from Lenin that she could use as ammunition. Rummaging at a barn sale I found a paperback entitled *The God That Failed,* an anthology of American writers and intellectuals who had become disillusioned with the Left. I paid the ten cents and bought it for her. That was the best bargain I ever got on a book, because for several years thereafter she presented me with a new book every Christmas.

What I saw in this girl—what I see again and again in young people that enables them to rebuild cathedrals and defy monkey-mimicking science teachers—was the ability to believe in something more than survival, gratification, and success. It was her having some conviction, aside from any content of the conviction itself, that I strove to reinforce. I think it was Toynbee who said that the values of Sparta and Valhalla are preferable to no values at all. And a misfired challenge to the young may be preferable to allowing their need for challenge and commitment to go unmet.

A couple of years ago, my colleague Bob Ketchum and I attempted to take our experience with student tutors and his experience in the Peace Corps one step further by using young people to teach adults in the community. If teenagers in Nicaragua could reduce illiteracy by tens of percentage points, why couldn't teenagers perform similar wonders in northeastern Vermont? And with the performance of even a dubious wonder, what questions might they be led to ask about democracy, education, and the meaning of a life? So we and a handful of students founded S.A.L.T.—Students and Adults Learning Together. Our members included my John Bircher and a very determined young man who would later join the Marines for some of the same reasons that he volunteered to be a Vermont *Brigadista*—because he believed he had a purpose beyond keeping fast food in his belly and gas in his car.

As a matter of prudence and courtesy—I hope not of timidity—we decided to begin by offering our services as auxiliaries to an adult-ed program already in place: we were welcomed, given mixed signals, stalled, then told before we had even begun that our services were not needed. William the Pig strikes again. The idea needs to rest awhile before being revived, and then we shall need to revive it more assertively—but that is not my point. My point is that a handful of Vermont teenagers were ready to give up lunch periods, after-school time, and weekends to tutor their neighbors, mind their tutored neighbors' kids, and take numerous risks, not least of all the risk of accomplishing nothing, and to make this commitment without the incentives of money, awards, privileges, or grades. Where we saw possibilities, they saw promise.

Working with students like these and like the boys who wrote *Born to Run*, I have come to the conclusion that the recent invention called adolescence appeals to them about as much as it appeals to me—not much at all. Puberty is beautiful; adolescence can be as cheap and trashy as the interests that prey upon it. As an idea, it is far more appealing to ten-year-olds who want to talk "dirty" and to certain thirty-five-year-olds who want to live the way the ten-year-olds talk. The hearts of most sixteen-year-olds are made of finer stuff. They do not want to be adolescents. They want to be young women and men. They believe in a promised land. And if we are not inclined to believe in something like the same thing, our every effort to help them amounts to a betrayal.

The Future Farmers of America

Here once the embattled farmers stood.

—EMERSON, "Concord Hymn"

I had a professor who during one of her digressions told us about a stint of high school teaching she had done in Kansas. I never determined which had disgusted her more, the job or the location, but I had no doubt that taken together they constituted the most dismal experience of her life. "On the first day of school," she said, "all of these kids walk into my class wearing dark blue corduroy jackets with the letters 'F.F.A.' on the back. I didn't even want to ask what they stood for. Does anyone here care to guess?" None of us did; she pronounced the F's as if they could have stood for one word only. "They stand for the Future Farmers of America . . . After a year, I was fortunate enough to leave Kansas and the Future Farmers of America forever."

Thanks to her, when I came to the Northeast Kingdom, I had with me, in addition to some erudite notes on Melville, the ability to recognize an F.F.A. jacket instantly. Soon I was able to meet the Future Farmers themselves, in classes and study halls, and when they came to my apartment to sell cider, citrus fruit, and maple syrup. With any luck I will never have to leave Vermont as my professor did Kansas; if I do leave, it will most likely be because the F.F.A. left before me.

17

My first real exposure to the organization came when I, my department head, and the principal were asked to serve as judges at the F.F.A. Creed Speaking Contest. The F.F.A. puts a great emphasis on public speaking, and it has a very practical reason for doing so. As a member of a rural community, a farmer will likely be called on to participate in self-government—more often and for higher stakes than his urban and suburban neighbors. In the Creed Speaking Contest one practices the elements of declamation by reciting expressively and from memory the F.F.A. Creed. Most of the participants will receive cash awards, and the best will then go on to district, possibly state competition.

The F.F.A. Creed

I believe in the future of farming, with a faith born not of words but of deeds—achievements won by the present and past generations of agriculturists; in the promise of better days through better ways, even as the better things we now enjoy have come to us from the struggles of former years.

I believe that to live and work on a good farm, or to be engaged in other agricultural pursuit, is pleasant as well as challenging; for I know the joys and discomforts of agricultural life and hold an inborn fondness for those associations which, even in hours of discouragement, I cannot deny.

I believe in leadership from ourselves and respect from others. I believe in my own ability to work efficiently and think clearly, with such knowledge and skill as I can secure, and in the ability of progressive agriculturists to serve our own and the public interest in producing and marketing the product of our toil.

I believe in less dependence on begging and more power in bargaining; in the life abundant and enough honest wealth to help make it so—for others as well as myself; in less need for charity and more of it when needed; in being happy myself and playing square with those whose happiness depends upon me.

I believe that rural America can and will hold true to the best traditions of our national life and that I can exert an influence in my home and community which will stand solid for my part in that inspiring task.

The contest would have been memorable in any event, but on that evening it was especially so for the efforts of a boy with cerebral palsy who said the creed with considerable unclearness and all the poignant intensity of a man expiring on a cross. The judges faced a dilemma in awarding the prizes. We seemed forced to choose between two evils of failing to recognize a superior effort, or patronizing it. We opted for the former, and I've never regretted our decision, though I drove home crying more bitterly than I have ever done since. I walked into the apartment barely able to explain my condition, poured myself a shot of whiskey from the "guests' " bottle in the pantry, swallowed it, and almost lost my large intestines through my nose. As the Future Farmers of America would be pleased to learn, I am normally a milk drinker, apparently for my own good.

In a calmer frame of mind, I was able to reflect on what I had seen that evening. For one thing, I was amazed and inspired by the atmosphere in which a boy with such difficulty in speech dared compete in, of all things, a speaking contest. Any teacher can tell you with what trepidation the average student views a speaking assignment. Were it not unsound pedagogy to threaten students with exercises in the skills we want them to master, we would have in the oral report a punishment more formidable than the dunce cap, the detention, and the hickory switch combined. Yet here was a young man for whom speaking was not only an embarrassing chore but also an outright handicap who felt able to give it a try before his principal, his teachers, and his assembled peers, some of whom are pretty rough characters. Certainly his willingness had much to say about his own extraordinary moxie. Perhaps, too, it had something to say about the chapter advisor, Mr. Randall, one of those men in whose presence anything cruel or foolish always looks exactly like what it is. But the willingness also had something to say about the F.F.A. itself, about its ideals and the strong solidarity among its members. One may mock a fellow inmate, even a fellow player, but one does not mock a comrade, a brother, and that was what this boy was to the rest of the club.

I was also impressed by the conduct of the meeting which preceded the Creed Speaking Contest. There was none of the self-consciousness, the giggling over mistakes, the "I'm above all this crap" glances that one might have expected in a formal meeting conducted by teenagers. Indeed, many a more "sophisticated" meeting would be put to shame by what I saw. I've sat in on legislative assemblies where the representatives moved or seconded motions like a man asking for his check in a diner where he has just eaten an undercooked egg. Here everyone seemed convinced of the importance of what he or she was doing, and of the necessity of doing it right. It comes as no surprise that when someone in the school community has a question on the proper conduct of meetings he or she goes not to the English teacher or to the history teacher or even to some member of the administration, but to the agriculture teacher who advises the F.F.A. And if he cannot answer the question, one knows he will not dismiss it by saying, "Nobody'll know the difference anyway."

Yet we know how close to right he'd be if he did say so. Last year at a school awards assembly the F.F.A. put on a short demonstration of parliamentary procedure, accelerating the process and adding some humor for the sake of holding interest. But the PA system was not working properly, and the acoustics in the gym (we have no auditorium) are poor. I looked up at the students sitting on the bleachers, many of whom appeared very puzzled. What on earth was it supposed to be, this blue corduroy machine with its members rising and chirping their motions and sitting back down again like the push rods in an old tractor engine? It's called democracy, boys and girls, and it will soon be replaced by something more efficient, that runs on microchips, libel, and cocaine.

Though well supported, the F.F.A. represents a minority of the student population, and certainly a minority in my classes, which are mostly for the college-bound. (It should be added that two of the most promising college-bound students in the school at this time are both active F.F.A. members.) The agriculture classes meet in the lowest level of the building, and while this is a matter of logistics more than of status—one can't very well drive a hay baler through a third-floor window—there is a more than architectural distinction between the basement and the so-called academic wing. Sometimes I tease my academic-wingers—and, I hope, compliment my Future Farmers—by asking the question: "If Socrates were to come to Lake Region Union High School today, what would he find the most comprehensible and/or laudable?" Given that the question pertains to no less a person than Socrates, the students know I consider it important. ("With Keizer it's either a Greek, a Jew, or that Johnson guy.") After looking up "laudable" in the dictionary, we begin.

No, Socrates would not necessarily have appreciated our reading of the Greek tragedies. In fact, he probably would have found *reading* a Greek tragedy about as purposeful as smelling a rock concert, though he would have readily admitted that there is something to be learned, however fragmentary, about dramas and rock concerts by reading and smelling respectively. No, not me, but thank you just the same; Socrates would have thought me too style-conscious and overdressed. Laughter—since by anyone's standards but Socrates', I am no such thing. Perhaps he would have had some slight understanding of your nagging me to hold classes outdoors in the good weather; he wouldn't have understood why we were indoors in the first place—that is, until an August frost bit his chiton.

What he really would have understood, though, is the Future Farmers of America. He would have understood it and liked it from the moment he walked into an F.F.A. meeting and saw the wooden owl, symbol of Athena, that sits before the advisor, and the image of Demeter's good grain in front of the chapter secretary. He would have admired the meetings, seeing in their conduct the cornerstone of the well-governed *polis*. He would have appreciated the F.F.A.'s fuzzy distinctions between vocational and academic, between academic and civic, between athletic and academic; he would have found it worthy of a philosopher's contemplation that the same organization was devoted to arm wrestling, declaiming speeches, pressing cider, and mowing the town cemeteries with equal enthusiasm. In the numerous judging competitions, for poultry, dairy cattle, beef, and cheese, he would have been delighted to see the marriage between talking well and knowing well what one is talking about, the prevalent estrangement of which would make much of our world an enigma to poor Socrates.

Of course Socrates will never come to Lake Region Union High School, at least not as a recognizable visitor, and all I have said is a matter of conjecture, possibly eccentric conjecture. My students are sharp enough to add the requisite grain of salt. But it is simply a fact, and one that all my students have heard, usually twice, that civilization begins with agriculture—that the *civitas* is not a possibility until farmers can produce enough food both to feed themselves and to liberate the mass of their neighbors from the task of food production and the deprivations of nomadic life. I wonder if anything I tell my students surprises some as much, or stays with some as long as this elementary historical principle—"no farms, no cities"—since they, like the rest of us, have come to regard rural and urban as opposites more than complements. "So," I tell them, "the next time the chic couple in the Volvo with New York plates goes whizzing past your farm on the way to some writers' conference or antique shop, with the two of them frantically rolling up the windows for fear of taking in a little whiff of manure, just remember, without the manure pile there can be no universities, no cathedrals, no theaters, no museums, no shopping malls, no courtrooms, no hospitals. Without the smell they're running from there's no Big Apple to run to. New York, San Francisco, Paris, Moscow, Rome—they're all sitting on giant piles of cow manure."

I don't have the heart to tell them that civilization will not collapse in one poetically just pile of shit should their parents be forced to sell out their farms to larger operators and brand their cows' faces for auction as beef. I don't have the heart to add that their avowed faith in "the ability of progressive agriculturalists to serve our own and the public interest in producing and marketing the product of our toil" has only served to make their betrayers rich. I don't have the heart to say that their question "How can farms be dying when so many people in the world and even right here are hungry?" though it may be morally astute and humanly answerable, makes as much economic sense within our present system as believing in a day when swords shall be beaten into plowshares and banks broken with a rod of iron.

I don't have the heart to tell them any of this, but when I see their faces so full of decency and hope, when I see them pull their blue corduroy jackets around their shoulders because it also makes scant economic sense to heat a school adequately when there are bombs to build, I want to tell everyone in this country how pathetically stupid we are. Stupid, stupid people. For in some sense our civilization *will fall* if the farms do—though we may not starve or need to forfeit our season tickets to whatever amusement preserves our vestigial awareness of the seasons. We may still have plenty of milk, but only at the cost of homogenizing our society. We will have lost something that gave our nation a part of its identity, and perhaps a disproportionate share of its integrity. Sandburg writes in his poem, "Chicago": "I have seen your painted women under the gas lamps luring the farm boys," and we are reminded how much, even of what we call urban, was made by farm kids who brought to the city their clear eyes and their blues. We are reminded of how much the life of small towns, the knowledge of animals, the reliance on the weather have formed our gadgets, our fictions, our hopes. I am not trying to write an elegy, or to deny what Marx once referred to as "the idiocy of rural life," of which I've seen my share. But I am saying that if we take the future away from the Future Farmers of America, we will have altered our future, too, by destroying our living continuity with the past.

Summers in this farm community end not so much with Labor Day as with the last fair. My wife and I are going to our last fair this afternoon. We always go to the animal barns first to see the best and most beautiful livestock in the county. To say that we will also see the best and most beautiful people sounds sentimental and contrived, but no one who has meandered in and out of the exhibition sheds would think so. All the generations are here, sitting on lawn chairs or hay bales, or else standing next to their animals, waiting for the call to show. The showing itself is done mainly by teenagers; all of them are dressed in white pants and shirts. The care of the show animals is also their responsibility, both here and at home. From reading some of their compositions, I know all that they have been doing for the past days and hours, carefully clipping the cow from forelock to udder in accordance with conventions set for each part, manicuring the hooves, cleaning out the ears, blow-drying the tail, milking the udder to its "correct" appearance of fullness, adjusting the cow's water and beet pulp feed to round but not bloat its middle, wiping off every splotch an animal might acquire in yards frequently soaked and muddy—a lot of work for a few cloth ribbons. But they hang their ribbons with pride over the immaculate stalls on which the animals' names are frequently enclosed in wreaths or hearts. It is Valentine's Day on Noah's ark, open house at the St. Francis Motel and Restaurant with draft horses, ponies, scores of varieties of rabbits, chickens, and vested sheep, a two-thousand-pound pink-bristled sow lounging in her stall like a goddess or a queen. We have brought our daughter; just potty-trained and always curious, she toddles over the straw repeating, "I want to see a cow make a poop." We meet several of my students, and they assure her that she has come to the right place. One of them picks her up and sits her astride a massive Holstein—she looks triumphant and a little trail sore, as if she has ridden the black-and-white cow all the way from her parents' an- cestral home in New Jersey to meet these kids. Somewhere deep in myself I give thanks that in a way she has. When I take her down, a boy hands us "I Love Milk" stickers, which we affix to our shirts, three more valentines in this kingdom of many and varied hearts.

Soon we will cross the racetracks to the screaming rides and greasy foods, the Black Sabbath T-shirts and the pickled deformities, the velvet icons of Elvis Presley and the stuffed pastel-colored animals, the games where "there's a winner every time," the girlie shows where "you get the strip without the tease"—we will move from the barns to the midway, as my professor moved from Kansas to New York City, as the farmers also move, if only for a weekend, to Burlington or Montreal to keep their balance and reappraise their peace. If it weren't for the fair's gaudy side, would I even bother to come? I'm not sure. But I know that there may come a time when I turn back from the midway, as so many do, with vomit in my throat and no money in my wallet, to rest my eyes in the barns' dim lights, to stroll one more time before going home past the lowing cattle and the couples snuggling in the hay and the farmers absorbed in their interminable debate upon the relative merits of Holsteins and Jerseys, arguing quietly so as not to wake their children—and I will find nothing but the night. Then I know for sure I will not come to the fair, perhaps for no other reason than that the night will soon swallow it all.

That's a grimmer conclusion than the Future Farmers of America would want for the chapter that bears their name, a grimmer conclusion, really, than local conditions may warrant. There are farmers elsewhere much worse off than many of ours. We have had a few foreclosures; a pig farmer farther south blew out his brains. So far the majority do not feel pressed enough (or is it solvent enough?) to join a national milk strike. But I know of some farm kids who feel pressed enough to lose sleep, who eat nothing but cheese sandwiches till the milk check comes, and who think that a college education is a rather unrealistic and selfish goal to have in times like these. And I know of one English teacher who can barely handle a martini cocktail, let alone a Molotov one, but who is nevertheless ready to volunteer his services should the F.F.A. move further underground than it already is.

Sex and Faith

It had all the marks of a Sunday School.

—*Huckleberry Finn*

*I*t used to be a truism that kids in the country became sexually aware at an early age because they saw farm animals copulate something like people. Now that television and the videocassette recorder have enabled kids everywhere to see people copulate something like farm animals, country kids are not so far ahead. But they have hardly fallen behind, for now they have VCRs *and* the rabbits. And, of course, they have the natural curiosity which teenagers have always had even when they lacked the current exposure.

Anyone who has ever taught youth has had cause to remark on the sexual preoccupation of his or her pupils. When the fifteen-year-old reading the part of Lady Macbeth tells her smirking husband "screw your courage to the sticking place"— this after one has harangued the class for twenty minutes on allowing the richness of Shakespeare's language to form images in the mind—one can readily anticipate the imagery that will form in certain minds when Macbeth gets his turn to say "Go prick thy face." I have read that Bertrand Russell advocated greater sexual freedom for his students in the belief that sexually satisfied young people would be better able to concentrate on their mathematics. One questions whether

Russell overestimated their tendency to distraction so much as their ability to be satisfied.

Anyone who teaches kids now will realize that their sexuality is more than the preoccupation it has always been— more, even, than the generally accepted pastime it has become. It is something like participation in a national religion that sees the aim, significance, and rewards of living as primarily sexual. Fear of AIDS and the recent talk about "safe sex" are no more a rejection of its dogmas than Calvinism was a rejection of Christianity. One does not have to be a teacher in order to recognize the religion, but a teacher may recognize it sooner than others, because a teacher always encounters piety at the age of indoctrination. And it is an obsessive and parochial kind of sexual piety that one finds oneself encountering in this society. I had a friend who claimed that an entire year's study of literature in the parochial school she attended consisted of memorizing which famous authors were Roman Catholic and which were not. She found this ridiculous, as do I, though I confess to the heresy of wondering how much less ridiculous it is to remember nothing more of Bach, Plato, or Catherine the Great than that the first sired twenty-odd kids, the second liked boys, and the third died trying to do it with a horse.

My students wonder how the people of Oceania could stand the sight of Big Brother flashed again and again in their faces; I wonder how my students can stand the no less frequent flashing of navels, crotches, and come-on looks in their own. Between the changes in their bodies and the unchanging face, or should I say rear end, of American popular culture, how much respite are they given from sexual stimulation? How prepared are they to evaluate a mythology in which heroes all have exceptionally varied and robust sex lives, and are perhaps heroic simply because they do; and reactionaries, hypocrites, and bogeymen are all perverted or celibate, perhaps perverted *because* celibate. We even blaspheme sexually.

In my youth, the Beatles dared say they were bigger than Christ; now we say that running gets us higher than sex, i.e., beyond the conceivable zenith of human experience. When my students find the moral universe of *The Scarlet Letter* alien, I am tempted to tell them that all they need do is turn Hester's badge upside down, make the "A" a "V," and think of Dimmesdale as the poor little girl in *The Breakfast Club* who must be forced into confessing that she is a virgin.

Such confessions come hard. "I really want to spend time with this guy," a girl writes, "and go out with him more than once, but I just don't feel like going to bed with him. I know that sounds weird." A cliché says that our society gives mixed signals to sexually developing young people. It is not mixed signals I see so much as the deadening certainty that I associate with a fundamentalist vision of the world. Mixed signals would be an improvement. Of course we do tell our kids that it's "OK to wait until you're ready" as we might tell them that it's OK to use your sleeve when you don't have a handkerchief or to be a leper when you don't have a choice. If we try to listen with their ears, I wonder, just how OK does our OK sound?

I don't wish to imply that my students have all swallowed what the culture feeds them about sex or anything else. If teachers know a thing about how kids are influenced, they know how incompletely and with what difficulty influence occurs. "Impressionable youngsters" are sometimes as impressionable as a block of granite. My students resist their culture as much or more than they resist their parents; often they resist both. What I am saying is that I see too many students feeling guilty about their resistance. I see too many being made to feel immature precisely because they have the maturity to recognize that they're still growing. Blaming that on peer pressure is like blaming atomic fallout on the wind; peer pressure simply carries what the whole culture drops on these kids by the megaton.

Finally, I am saying that too many of my students get pregnant. I hate our sexual religion because my desk sits under the drain that takes the blood from its altars. And my desk sits in a drier spot than some others, for I teach the "upper" levels, the slightly better dressed, the college-bound, or in the case of my few young mothers, those who might have been college-bound.

Dealing with a student who is pregnant or a mother is, for me, like offering condolences to the bereaved; it is something I shall never do well. Perhaps my efforts at both are undermined by a sense of what shouldn't be: that our parents shouldn't die, that our children shouldn't be parents. Paradoxically, I am also made uneasy by remembering that in comparison with other societies and other eras, it is I and my kind who are aberrant, not the teenaged mothers.

Yet aberrant they remain—no matter who looks at them. For they are both the products and the pariahs of our sexual religion. By having and proving sexual intercourse, they show themselves fervent "believers." At the same time, by reaffirming a connection between sexuality and reproduction, and by forfeiting some of their share of erotic opportunity, they are heretics of the worst mark. Hester Prynne and Tess Durbeyfield were stigmatized as examples of ungoverned sensuality; there is something contrastingly chaste but equally stigmatized in the image of a pregnant girl standing by her locker at school.

I try to be helpful. I try to juggle notions of maternity leave, course continuity, and fairness to the unpregnant portion of the class when making homework assignments. I drop hints about prenatal or infant care when I think those hints are needed. "Of course you know about alcohol." I try to be responsive to the almost pathetic yearning and the often incredible tendency of these girls to be very good mothers.

And I try to be optimistic; at least I try to be encouraging, to keep alive some faith in possibilities. You may have chosen to be a teenaged mother, but that does not mean that you must do all the things that others have done who made the same choice. "Two roads diverged in a yellow wood" begins a nice poem, but roads in the world crisscross as much as they diverge, and you do not have to stay on this exit forever.

I once walked a road in a yellow wood with a student, four or five months pregnant, who had not returned to school for her junior year. I urged her not to drop out. There was home study that could be arranged, there were deals that could be made—there was time. It was only October. I cited an example.

"Do you remember the Harris girl—Judy? Do you know her?"

"Yeah, I know her."

"Well then, you know Judy got pregnant when she was just a year older than you. And she had her baby, and she got married—in fact, I think she just had another, a little girl—but she stayed in school and she finished. She did her work; she even did more than I had asked. When she came home from the hospital she had done as much writing as some of the kids in class. And the thing is, she was a smart girl, but you've got a lot more ability even than she had, at least in English. I know you could swing it. You may be saying 'That's all well and good, but so what if I can? It doesn't have anything to do with where I'm at now.' Maybe it doesn't. But think ahead a year or five years, or whatever. You might want a job, and as impossible as it might sound, you might want to go to college. And I'm not just saying think about yourself and *your* future and *your* talents and all of that. I am saying think about those things—they're important to think about—but that's not all I'm saying. I'm also saying think about your kid and your . . . the kid's father and the three of you and your relationship with each other

and how you're going to survive. If you've got an education . . . I mean, let's say that Judy and her husband
wanted—"

"Do you know Judy's husband?" she asked.

"No I don't. He's quite a bit older than she is. I wasn't
teaching here when he was in school. Why do you ask?"

"He's my baby's father."

All the more reason to finish school, but I don't say it.
Questioning the reliability of a kid's lover, or of anyone else's
for that matter, is almost always futile. And at that point I
was too busy trying to reason myself out of a fantasy in which
social work was done by firing squad. I urged her once more
to come back to school. She said she'd think about it. My
good-bye was more casual than it would have been had I
known that I was never to meet with her again.

In the past two years I have been a parent myself. Interestingly enough, this has not made me any less awkward with
my student mothers. It has made me more accessible to them,
however. They come with photographs and anecdotes. I know
that I have set myself up for this. I talk quite frequently about
my daughter, in part because I'm an all-too-typical father,
and in part because I want my students to know all that is
involved in parenting, and I want my boys to know that it's
OK—there's that word again—that it's more than OK, that
it's fine and dandy and wonderful for a man to like babies
and to change their diapers. At least that is how I rationalize
passing around a photograph now and then. So the girls come
up to the desk after class with their pictures, and I make an
unfeigned fuss over them, not neglecting to drop my pediatric
hint for the day. "This is cute . . . ah, does the baby always
have a chocolate bar for snack?" I suppose the fuss and the
comment come under the heading of support; I suppose that
a "supportive" teacher is supposed to do such things. Yet I
wonder, what insecure girl waits her turn at the desk to talk
to me about an introductory paragraph or an unfamiliar

abbreviation and thinks to herself, This kid in front of me is a parent. She has to do her homework just like me, but she is a parent, and so a peer to the teacher, who is also a parent. If I became a parent . . .

She doesn't hear the voice inside me that is shouting "A chocolate bar! Do you realize . . . I'm thirty-three years old with a wife as old and as educated as myself and the two of us need all the energy and know-how we've got to take proper care of our kid, and you're three years past believing in the tooth fairy and your kid just got his first tooth? And you're celebrating that with a chocolate bar! How could you let this happen to you? And where's the bum who's supposed to be this kid's father? What's he doing?"

Sometimes what he's doing is helping to raise the child. Just as often, he's not. It's a simplistic thing to say, but it can seem as if we told our young women that their role is not defined as that of babymaker and victim, and they did not believe us; and we told our young men that their role is not defined as that of provider and protector, and they did. In one anonymous poll I asked a class's opinion on legalized abortion. The boys were almost unanimously in favor; the girls, sharply divided. Of course this was one sloppy poll in one small class. But I wondered about the boys. Was the vote their recognition of a girl's rights or their tendency to stay out of "a girl's affairs"? Were they acknowledging the decision of a pregnant woman as inviolate or her pregnancy as irrelevant?

However they acknowledge it, the rest of us need to recognize that a number of our teenage pregnancies are deliberate. They are cases of planned parenthood. Most of our young mothers knew about contraception beforehand; a few were receiving contraceptives free of cost. The causes of their pregnancy have less to do with ignorance of reproduction, contraception, or the demands of parenting than with things like the desire to establish the first stable relationship in one's life, the desire to have something important and indisputably one's own, the need to get out of one's house. Probably more than one girl has had her boyfriend's baby as a preferable alternative to having her father's. All of this bespeaks a society in which women have too little status and an economy in which rural people have too little justice. But we would rather deal with contraception than the former, and we would rather deal with almost anything—even AIDS—than the latter. It is much easier to provide a girl with a bogus prescription for birth control pills than it is to provide her mother with a well-paying job. And it is much easier for the girl to neglect to take her pill than it is for her to ignore what television, radio, and cinema are intoning day after day in a ceaseless litany, not only about "good sex," but also about a "good life" which has no place for her need and little need of her contributions.

There is no question that the girl could use a healthy dose of feminism, or that it would be helpful to teach her about sexual equality even in the face of economic inequality. I have begun to notice the cost of sexism in places I had never thought or cared to look for it before. For example, the grades of boys with a steady girl often improve; the grades of girls in the same situation tend to remain constant or go down. These are casual observations, not a summary of hard statistics, but they point to a need. The near starvation of two anorexic female students probably points to the same need. Nevertheless, one minded to meet the need encounters two obstacles, aside from the prejudice of a society that remains by and large patriarchal.

The first is that in spite of many disclaimers and some noteworthy exceptions, the model for feminism which most of us "laypersons" have learned is adversarial and exclusive. I don't know if we have recognized how utterly it fails with the average teenager. One may get the girls to maintain that "women are just as good as men" in that stick-our-tongues-out sort of way, but young men and women care too much about each other's acceptance to risk much more. I once asked a class in one of my innumerable polls how they felt about the principle of equal pay for equal work. Unanimously they were in favor. I asked how many would consider voting for a woman President. Most would. I asked how many would consider themselves feminists. One sharp boy got his hand a few inches off the desk, looked at the vacancy all around him, and figured what was the use. If the fight against sexism at the high school level needs anything, it needs models based on camaraderie—such as those we see in countries where men and women reflect on their shared experience of a revolutionary struggle. Young men and women make much better comrades in arms than they do cynics in bed. This is why I think we can hardly underestimate the importance of nonsexist athletic programs in the school. If a healthier and more just relationship between the sexes is ever to come to our society, I think it is likelier to come from girls and boys running around the same cinder track, sharing their gum and their glory, than from jaded men and women sitting around in the same kind of segregated klatches, sharing their bitterness.

The other obstacle, not so much to feminism per se as to feminism's ability to provide our young people with an effective critique of such things as teenage pregnancy and sexual coercion, is that in a culture whose values are so ponderously sexual, liberation of the sexes is quite narrowly defined. As commonly understood, it comes much closer to Hugh Hefner's priorities than it does to Betty Friedan's. The popular connotation of "liberated" is often little more than "promiscuous." One wonders how far we've come from the days when "adventurer" meant "doer of bold deeds" and "adventuress" meant "slut." Have we finally admitted that the adventurous woman can be a knight, or merely admitted the "slut" to knighthood—granted that both may be nice things to do? In any case, though I have no poll to cite, I'd imagine that for many of my students the image projected by Madonna, say, represents a more "liberated" woman than Winnie Mandela.

Maybe they're right. Maybe I don't know what I'm talking about. One need only read the letters for two weeks following the review of a book on women's studies in the *Times* to conclude that hardly anyone knows what she's talking about and certainly no one knows what he's talking about when we talk about the sexes. But I cannot talk for long. One redeeming fact about being a high school teacher is that you are too busy to take your own abstract thinking very seriously, and too lowly regarded for anyone else to.

And so I adopt a course of action based on a few things I think are right. The program and the results will both be modest, however grandiose the thinking behind them. I urge students to read biographies of women. If they have trouble finding a suitable biography, I help them ask why. I do grammar lessons where the antecedent of the pronoun "she" is doctor, lawyer, or Indian chief. I send a class to work in groups with the warning: "I better not see female secretaries in more than half of these teams." I send my girls to college with the admonition: "Learn to recognize the professor who gets his jollies out of trying to make you blush; learn to stare the bastard down."

I hope without being too precious I try to widen my students' conception of acceptable male activity, realizing that this is often a trick of maintaining credentials in one world in order to speak in another. Perhaps I talk about how pesty it is to vacuum up the wood chips I track in from the chain saw. I avoid treating my boys with that overbearing top-rooster manner which serves both to make them feel emasculated and to confirm all the worst images of masculinity. And I try never to court my girls in the guise of the Sensitive

Male English Teacher (S.M.E.T.). There is a special circle in hell reserved for Sensitive Male English Teachers.

As one corrective, I teach myself the discipline of allowing girls to cry (not of making them cry) without shame but without benefit. This has been a hard one for me, since my natural reaction to the sight of anyone in tears is the impulse to rend my garments. But I am learning.

I've found my vision of the need for toleration and justice between the sexes and among the members of one sex expanding, led not so much by the range of my thoughts as by the laughter of my class—not a bad way to be led. Every spring my freshman scholars begin Hardy's *Return of the Native* with a snicker as the rustics of Egdon Heath celebrate Guy Fawkes Day by burning bundles of faggots. (Eustacia Vye's indiscretions notwithstanding, this is one book the Moral Majority will never seek to ban.) And so we begin to talk about denotations and connotations, about stereotypes, and such old-fashioned traditional values as common courtesy. "How do you know," I ask them, "that the kid sitting next to you is not a 'faggot'? It's like your vulgar word 'retard'— how do you know that someone here doesn't have a brother or sister who's mentally retarded? How must it feel to hear such a word said over and over again in that way? You know, its been said that an average of one out of every ten men is gay. There are twelve boys in this class, thirteen males counting me." Pause. "That means it's perfectly possible that one man here is gay."

A waggish statistician in the back of the room raises his hand. "Nah, I don't think it's any of us, Mr. Keizer. There must be *two* of them in the other class."

Without mentioning a name, I tell them of a gay student I had, tall and strong—"you wouldn't have gotten away with calling him a sissy." And I think to myself of his letter; at the time he was stationed near San Francisco—"not minding the Service at all"—and would soon be sailing north to "someplace called the Illusion Islands." Like most of us, gay or straight, male or female, he will find his illusions chillier than expected, but I wish him well in his life, and I say so out loud to the class.

I do not as yet say anything about the courage, the compassion, and the suffering of another boy—short and frail this time—who hated nothing in his life so much as being a boy. But how I wish some of my students could have sat in on our first conference, which he requested only hours after I had lectured in Bible as Literature on "The Parables and the Outcasts," and have heard some of what it means, not to be one in ten, but to be one in hundreds of thousands. I wish they and their parents, too, could have read his final exam, where he discusses the words of Jesus telling his disciples to love their enemies, and yet to shake from their feet the dust of a town that rejects them.

I suspect that more than most high schools, ours is one where future spouses meet. Most of our kids don't have to get married; they want to get married, but they often get married nearly as young as those who have to. One watches the solemn march to the podium at graduation; shortly thereafter, one may be invited to witness the solemn march to the altar. Both occasions are so full of hope, a hope enhanced even as it is symbolically challenged by the brevity of summer and by the coming winter's brutality.

In the middle of July—a month ago as I write—I go to St. John of the Cross Church in East Albany for the wedding of two former students. I arrive early, I sit in the last pew. The church is cool and clean and bright, reflecting sensibilities both Catholic and Yankee, with freshly painted white walls and several polychrome statues of the saints in white niches. On one side of me is a young father, sleeves rolled up over his tattooed forearms, and on the other an elegant family of three who would seem to have cut short their vacation in Nantucket, or wherever. In front of us, a farmer, or what I take for a farmer, with long sideburns and an amazing tie. And all up the pews the whole motley, lovely Northeast Kingdom appears to be gathering, smiling expectantly, facing a nine-foot crucifix which seems no more incongruous with the joy of the occasion than the cuff links do with their wearers' roughened hands. So I am already in an apocalyptic frame of mind before the bride appears and the priest begins to speak of the Mystical Marriage.

I don't know if any couple I have taught ever impressed me more with their regard for one another, with the way they look like a couple, with their chances to survive as such. He is a tall, rugged gentleman, holder of the school discus record, a carpenter for the year since his graduation, almost more quiet than the bride. She has just taken her diploma. Though her plans have been known for some time, in her white gown and dark beauty she is more bride than I could have imagined. She will go to work at a good secretarial position for which I wrote a letter of recommendation that read like a manifesto. Both she and I know the letter I wanted to write in its stead.

With all the reasons I could muster, I urged her to think of college, not to turn away from her relationship or even from her wedding plans, but to integrate them somehow with plans for further study. She was the only student in my first-semester expository writing class to receive an A—though she paid for it in numerous revised drafts and a lot of tiresome advice. "Construction is just booming down by the university. I know he'd have no trouble finding work. If you took a lighter load, you'd have most evenings free. You might be able to qualify for some money. My wife and I were students in the first years of our marriage"—on and on. I have come here, then, to witness their wedding and to confirm, at least for the present, the failure of my good intentions.

There was hardly a doubt in my mind that I would fail. I was butting my head against that force which the words "romantic" and "erotic" each in their way misname. It keeps us from concentrating on our mathematics. Were there another force as great to overcome, the Buddha said, he would never have reached enlightenment. It keeps us from that too. But for all the pious and reductionistic rubbish that our culture has made from it, what a lot of rubbish it destroys; what a lot of cant it grinds to powder. Sometimes I fantasize a great school assembly to which all the social prognosticators of our time have been invited—those who say the family is dead or must die, those who say it surely will die, and all of human nurturing with it, if we do anything so foolish as pass an Equal Rights Amendment or light the Guy Fawkes bonfires with anything but faggots—and as I look over the audience, I notice that half its members are too busy passing love notes and fondling one another to pay any attention, and I am too busy laughing to make them behave. Surely there must be times when the sculptor laughs for joy at the hardness of the stone. It rejects his accidental blows as well as his intentional ones; it resists time as much as art. I am thankful for the stone that foils me, often for my own and others' good, and I am thankful for my proximity as a teacher to the stone at its best and hardest, in the young. But I doubt I look like a thankful man there in the church, more like one struggling to hold his bowels, as I try to keep back my tears.

Now the groom kisses the bride, and the veil that has been coming undone all during the service falls at last, like a curtain, and this time her nervous hands cannot prevent it. I congratulate husband and wife on my way out of the church and thank them for inviting me. I wish both good luck. In several months I'll meet them in the grocery store and I'll just mention college; it can't hurt. For now I have another person to meet before I return home.

I am going to say good-bye to someone who is only a few

days away from shaking the dust of a small Vermont town from his feet. He may soon learn that in our society gender is a tougher thing to shake than dust or men's clothing; he is already learning how much he will miss certain neighbors whose kindness he will leave with the dust. Though the mood of the meeting contrasts strongly with the wedding before, it is tinged with a similar faith.

"You're worried about me, aren't you?" he says.

"You bet your life I'm worried. I'm *extremely* worried."

"Well, don't be. I know it sounds ridiculous, but I know inside myself that even though there's going to be pain in my life—I know that everything will turn out well in the end."

I am hoping he is right, in more ways than either of us can fathom, for more people than either of us can know, as I drive home with a blue crepe streamer flying from my antenna, past glacial lakes, and horny farm animals, and mountains older than the groin.

Courtesy

Grace works to uplift, to reward, and ever to surpass all we desire
or deserve. In this way it makes known and displays the supreme,
many-sided generosity of God . . . and his exquisite courtesy.

—DAME JULIANA OF NORWICH

My wife tells the story of the way she and another
little girl decided to punish a wife-beater who lived across
the street. The two playmates were outraged by the woman's
black eye, so when they saw her husband working out in his
yard, they walked to the edge of the driveway in which they
had been jumping rope and stood for the better part of a half
hour silently pointing at the man. Pointing at another person,
they had been taught, is extremely impolite.

One's first response to the story is to smile at the fond
schemes of childhood. A more thoughtful response is to realize that had the entire town shown the wisdom of two little
girls, it might never have known a case of domestic abuse
again. But what strikes me about the story today is how much
a sense of courtesy had been impressed on the two children.
The most drastic thing they could think to do was to breach
it. It sometimes seems as though all I learned in first grade
was how to read and how to be polite. If so, I was well
taught.

What has impressed me most about the kids I teach—more

than some of their grammatical abominations, more than all the chores some of them do before they come to school—is their overall good manners. My students would probably be amazed to hear me say so, in view of my constant corrections of the same. But when allowances have been made for what we expect from young people these days, and for the way in which an institutional setting can bring out the worst in human beings, my students are a touchingly courteous bunch.

Note that I am talking about courtesy, not etiquette. Although the two can certainly overlap, I see the first as essentially an ethical concern; the latter, an aesthetic one. The first grows out of the recognition that everybody has a right to be here; the latter can grow out of a belief that everybody has no such thing, and can be the means of discovering who was let in by mistake. At its worst, etiquette is a form of discourtesy. My students do sometimes show an ignorance of etiquette even at its best, and we probably do well to familiarize them with its generally accepted rules. Right now, for instance, there's been a clamping down on boys wearing their caps indoors. I go along with the injunction, though for my own part I can tolerate a hat in a public building providing that the wearer can say "thank you" and keep his voice down. Actually I've come to regard feed caps and those with chain saw logos as a kind of Northeast Kingdom yarmulke; I had thought of wearing one indoors myself as a show of goodwill and respect.

Most people would agree that our society could stand to be more courteous, that our young are often not courteous; but in this as in other concerns, where "most people would agree" is also where many people have given up. Courtesy, like craftsmanship and commitment, is one of those qualities we lament the death of but seem in no great hurry to resurrect. My own narrow conception of etiquette may well be but one more symptom of a culture which advertises its cars and perfumes as "bold and brassy." Perhaps soon the advertisers will themselves be bold and brassy enough, and honest enough, to say "shameless and obnoxious." Then we will have brought our youth-oriented culture to fulfillment, praising our products with the same words we use to describe our young.

Why any of this should be, I don't know, but I am convinced that rudeness works downward to the young instead of upward from them. I also think that for some people courtesy has an unpleasant suggestion of inefficiency about it. It carries echoes of a royal "court," with its antiquated customs, or court-ship, another thing we've outgrown; it means serving, and waiting, and putting your own wants on hold; it's "After you, my dear Alphonse" and "After you, my dear Gaston" when it would be so much more to the point just to barrel on through and hope that dear Alphonse has enough sense to get back up before the door swings into his head. At least that is the rationale I imagine when I'm in a restaurant or checkout line with some summer visitor who's obviously been sitting in his or her rented cottage all week reading one of those books on the merits of intimidation. Why all these trivial considerations, one can hear the author say, when all you need to know is what you want and how to get it? It's something like the question "Why all these miserable little farms when all we need is one big high-tech agribusiness?" Both bespeak our love affair with precision, speed, and "what works for me"—our love affair with ourselves.

Most of my students were born during the so-called "ME decade," and many of them are direct heirs of that earlier movement which reduced all ethics *and* etiquette to the maxim "Anything I do is all right so long as it doesn't hurt somebody else." It wasn't a bad maxim, I think, except that in practice it usually carried the corollary "And if, perchance, anything I do *does* hurt somebody else, that is because somebody else has a *very* big problem." Hence our question "What's *your* problem?" which, if there was any way to know such things, I would bet has been said fewer times to rude people than to people flinching in the face of rudeness. Whenever I hear a kid in my classroom say it, I know that something bold and brassy is just around the corner. Nevertheless, despite their inheritance, my students remain, as I have said, a basically courteous group. For along with the influences named above come others contrary but no less powerful, some regional, some ethnic, some owing to that bedrock decency a teacher must believe inheres in every human being. When I enter the school building with arms full and three kids grab the door and my bundles, I must believe that there is hope for the twenty-first century, or else that I have been caught somehow in the nineteenth. No doubt there are good reasons for believing both.

Where my students seem to need help in becoming *more* courteous is in two areas. We tend to regard both as the natural weaknesses of teenagers, but they are, in fact, weaknesses we share as a culture.

The first has to do with respect for privacy. Teenagers can be an extremely nosy group of people. They want to know what their neighbor got on his test, why she was called to the office, why he's smiling, why she's crying, how much he weighs, where she got her hickey. A teacher sometimes has all that he or she can do not only to protect the privacy of some suddenly fascinating individual, but also to prevent these interests from disabling larger ones. In the end, respect for another's privacy is often a sign of the recollectedness with which we attend to our own tasks and vision. A student's loss of that recollectedness can be as frustrating to a teacher as a show of bad manners. For example, when I tell a class an anecdote similar to those I've scattered throughout this book, what I often get by way of response is "Who was it? What was the kid's name?" In their rush to identify the character they run right past the whole story's point.

Well, that's just teenagers, we say. Is it? At the time of this writing, the world has been privileged to discover some hitherto unknown paintings by Andrew Wyeth. I like what I know of Wyeth's work, and I like what I've seen of these paintings, many of them nudes. Why the intimate details of the model's biography or the painter's marriage should prove of greater interest than the mystical marriage of the model's anatomy and the painter's talent is quite beyond me. But do the articles in our national magazines help me to grasp the full significance of that latter marriage—do they enable me and other artistic illiterates to understand all that makes one of these nudes transcendently different from a *Playboy* centerfold with its trite little vita: "Helga likes windsurfing, panda bears, and sangria, and may have just thrown a big monkey wrench into Andrew Wyeth's marriage"? If I'm not one of the Wyeths, why should I care, and what right have I to know?

We live in a time when our right to know everything we require to satisfy our needs as a self-governing people has subtly been translated into our *right* to know everything we require to satisfy our most prurient curiosities. A teacher who tells his or her class to mind its own business, to let the failing marriage of a student's parents or the failing grade on a student's paper be his own affair, had better understand that in the minds of many students the teacher is violating a right rather than upholding one. He or she had better think of the task not so much as one of gentle redirection as one of militant iconoclasm. That is certainly how I think of it, as I smash away.

The other area where we need to work on courtesy might be called courtesy's second half, if the first half is considered a respect for individual privacy. This has to do with respect for what we all share, for public domain, environment, atmosphere, silence. For silence above all. I've always thought it strange to send a kid home from school for filling the bathroom with a little cigarette smoke, when we merely scold a kid for filling libraries and lecture halls with a barrage of distracting noise.

I imagine some would find *me* strange for thinking this way. I also imagine that if one asked my students, "Does Mr. Keizer have any special peculiarities?" most would answer that, aside from tripping over the wastebasket during lectures, Mr. Keizer's single greatest quirk is his mania for silence. Students and teachers both come into the study halls I monitor whispering, "Is this a class?" The question reveals more, I think, than the strictness with which I keep a study hall. It seems to presuppose that while interruptions of a teacher's work "in class" are rude and counterproductive, interruptions of a student's private study or reading are somewhat expected. No, they're not. I tell my students they have as much right to demand quiet during their individual studies as their teachers do during a final exam. I tell them that they have a right to demand a quiet place to work in their households—that every family member has that right—and that I will talk to their parents myself if their own petitions fail to be heard over the television. Finally, I tell them that my vision for their school, as well as my definition of a true "study *hall*," will be revealed when students knock on my classroom door and ask politely if I might lecture at a somewhat lower volume so as not to distract from their studies out in the hall. On that day, I tell them, I will go out into the hall myself and sit on the floor with the scholars. School will have begun at last.

Most students' violations of their neighbors' silence, even most of the litter and some of the defacement we see in a school, are innocent enough. They result from thoughtlessness or boredom more than from deliberate viciousness. They also point to a value system in which public property is perceived as far less sacred than private property. Most of the kids who spray-paint obscenities and valentines on the bridge abutments or scrawl them in a public lavatory would not think of doing the same to a private home. They believe, like most of their fellow Americans, that what belongs to one of us is infinitely more important than what belongs to us all. In one sense, the public bathrooms and the bridge abutments will never get cleaner as long as we believe that purse snatchers are more nefarious than air-polluters, or that each of us ought to have new living room carpets before the school can have a new gym floor.

Of course there is a point at which the litter has not been dropped so much as aimed, where the phantom messages on public walls become too boundless and bizarre—and we feel not so much disrespected as assaulted by those who put them there. I took my daughter to play in a beautiful park in a little town not far from where we live. I was going to give her a penny to toss into the fountain, but there were too many wishes that had been made before ours, with bottle caps, cigarette butts, and broken glass. I thought of Holden Caulfield in *The Catcher in the Rye,* outraged to see "fuck you" written where "little kids would see it." I thought of the gum and chewing tobacco spit into the drinking fountains at school. What makes someone throw garbage into a fountain, if not a rapist kind of mentality—a need to inspire feelings of helplessness and disgust in another person, a sick desire to force a painful acknowledgment of one's own power and presence on the earth?

My fountain can serve as a metaphor of the two ways a teacher can regard a class when thinking on the matter of courtesy. The first is to ask: Which one of these little bastards would dump garbage into a fountain? The other is to ask: Which of these kids is a fountain into which a load of garbage has been dumped? We need to tell ourselves over and over that school is the first place where many students will encounter both a sense of public domain and a sense of personal worth. We need to tell our students, as I tell all of my freshmen on the first day of high school, that each of them is sacred and that they have just walked into a sacred space.

That means that no one is mocked, no one is ignored, no

one's right to learn or to work fruitfully and with dignity is violated or abridged. It means there are no nerds, no queers, no retards, no people known by the name of their genitals, no genitals known by their names on the street, few untouchable subjects, but above all, no untouchable people. We don't "make an effort" to be courteous; we simply are. Ignorance is tolerable, shyness is tolerable, anger is tolerable, challenges to the teacher are tolerable and sometimes praiseworthy, but willful impertinence in this classroom is not only intolerable, it does not even exist. Sometimes we may *think* we see rudeness, but the rudeness or the person performing it vanishes so quickly that we cannot be sure we saw anything at all. And if life in such an environment becomes too ho-hum, and needs a touch of danger, then harass a thirty-dollar-a-day substitute to the verge of tears, and life here will become dangerous beyond your wildest dreams.

Admonitions such as these are not incidental to the core curriculum; they are very much at the core. They have less to do with "laying down the law" than they do with breaking up the ground in order to plant for intellectual growth. For while courtesy may have to be established with a little dread, it is perfected by empathy, and empathy is an act of the creative imagination. How can we expect our students to understand what it means to be Oliver Twist or Quasimodo if we haven't even demanded that they understand what it means to be an exploited substitute or a kid with too many pimples? How can they grasp that it is not Hamlet's "job" to die young, but only a tragic consequence of his destiny, if they cannot understand that it is not the janitor's "job" to pick up dropped orange peelings, only one of the unsavory consequences of his job description? "How would you feel if a man walked into your father's barn, pulled down his pants, defecated in the aisle, and then said 'With all the manure in this place, I just figured it was your job to dispose of mine'?" Have a student take his or her orange peelings to the wastebasket with that question in mind before you send him or her to *Medea* or *The Grapes of Wrath* with any question more abstract.

The teacher who would make his or her classroom a school for courtesy must remember not only that he or she is its chief exemplar, but also that he or she is very likely to be its first violator. Whereas students are impeded by carelessness, the teacher is impeded by his or her own power, and it may well be that the latter is a more serious impediment. One can make the case that our whole concept of courtesy is rooted etymologically and historically in Western man's first attempts to restrain *power* both in political and in erotic relationships. A teacher, then—at least the teacher speaking here—needs to be careful lest his efforts at enforcing courteous behavior lead to the reinforcement of its opposite.

I try to make my point in simple things. I avoid sharing anything with a class that a student would want shared with himself or herself alone. I avoid writing comments on top of a student's writing, or putting a grade on top of a student's name. We work one-to-one, not one-*on*-one. I ask permission before quoting from a composition, before marking up a draft in conference, before tearing a page out of a student's notebook or looking at any page therein. I try to be certain that no student stands for any length of time while I sit. And when I have observed all of these minutiae, only to offend on a grosser scale, I apologize, privately if the offense was private, publicly if public. Sometimes I am led to wonder if there are kids in my class who have been compelled to say "I'm sorry" hundreds of times but who have hardly ever had the same said to them. If I knew who they were, I almost think I might offend them deliberately in some small way, just so they might be able to forgive me when I came, feed cap yarmulke in hand, to beg their pardon.

With all of its opportunities for trespass, with all of its peculiar relationships, a school is a good place for younger and older people to discover the pleasure of reciprocal acknowledgment, which is what courtesy is, and if we listen to certain poets and mystics, what heaven is, too, and what earth is meant to be: each creature expressing its appreciative awareness of every other, each being restraining itself for a time so that in time all may be themselves without stint, diminution, or shame. Undoubtedly school never becomes Eden. And the real test of courtesy is probably not how it mirrors some paradise, but how it survives in a world rank with shame, and shamelessness, and noise. Strangely enough, the example of courtesy I recall most often was an act of violence. Perhaps that only illustrates how imperfect I am in courtesy. But the young man in my example was as near to perfect courtesy as anyone I ever met.

I'll call him Pierre. He was a type often overlooked when we talk on things "Yankee"—a French Catholic farm kid from a large family with children from toddlers to twenty-year-olds where there is a great emphasis on manners, cleanliness, respect for authority, and family strength, but also a jocularity and a sensual joy that prevent any of this from being priggish or stern.

Pierre had an older brother who came to high school *after* he did. The brother's academic problems, a slight stutter and the fact that he was larger than most students, including Pierre, but also more awkward, made him the ideal target for a bully. He was "fair" game—he could hardly say "Pick on somebody your own size"—but safe game, too.

One morning before the homeroom bell, Pierre, whom I have never heard mock, taunt, or swear, decided to confront his brother's tormentor. "You've been picking on my brother," he said. "I'd like you to stop." The bully was greatly amused. "Are you going to make me fight you?" Pierre asked, without bluster, without any wish to fight.

"Why don't you ask me again?" said the boy.

I'm told the latter went down with one punch and that

several moments passed before his eyes unglazed. I'm also told that a teacher "saw the whole thing," but like Pierre, he was no novice in matters of courtesy. Someone had apparently taught him that there are moments of human tenderness, even of violent tenderness, when a gentleman averts his eyes. He stepped into his homeroom while Pierre, never one to be late or to hit a man who's down, walked quietly back to his.

Parents

I have a small
daughter called
Cleis, who is

like a golden
flower
    I wouldn't
take all Croesus'
kingdom with love
thrown in, for her

—Sappho

I have in mind a monument that can stand in any park
or green of the nation. It depicts a man and a woman seated
at a table on top of which towers an indescribable monstrosity, half mechanical and half alive, with propellers, bug eyes,
smokestacks, and mandibles all over it. The man and woman
are holding various tools and weapons, and appear very concerned. At the side of the table stands a child. In some versions
the monstrosity is replaced by an enormous globe, which is
clearly too large to be a globe, and is meant to stand for the
whole world; here the man and woman appear godlike, but
no less concerned, and the child may have wings. But in all
versions the inscription at the base of the monument is the
same. It reads: "The kid needed it for school."

Until such time as I can convince or commission someone

to sculpt this, my purpose will have to be served by a twelve-inch model of Polyphemos the Cyclops which stands on top of my filing cabinet. He has a clay face and body, a marble for an eye, and surprisingly lifelike hair and beard. The boy who brought it in explains: "We were all working on it together, but nobody knew what to do for the hair. Then all of a sudden, Mom reaches out and muckles on to the cat . . ." When I feel the demands of my job insupportable, or when I need a warmer vision of the human race, I sometimes look into Polyphemos' mystic eye and picture in my mind this hardworking farm family, whom I have come to love a great deal, saddled not only with the weight of February snow and the Dairy Termination Program, but with the dilemma of twin sons each of whom needs a project based on classical Greek literature, and it's due tomorrow ("The time kind of got away from us")—I see them toiling together in this as in all else, even Fluffy or whatever the cat's name is being called upon to make her sacrifice and become less fluffy for a higher good. "There, there, Fluffy, he needed it for school."

Every so often a teacher remembers that all of his or her students have parents or guardians, those people who help with the projects, read the report cards, and, we most earnestly hope, pay their property taxes. Living in a rural community, I suppose that I see more of students' parents than do teachers in other places. The man who pumps gas into my car, the woman who cashes my paycheck, the man who fills my prescriptions, the woman who checks out my groceries, the man who delivers the propane fuel, our lawyer, our family doctor, my principal, the school custodian, the school secretary, the school cooks, and several of my teacher colleagues are all parents of students or of former students. I think we have developed a fair code of ethics by which parent-proprietor and teacher-customer share information, mostly positive information, without making parent, teacher, *or* student wish that he or she lived somewhere else.

Yet, in spite of this familiarity with many parents, things like back-to-school nights always come with a bit of a jolt. To begin with, I'm surprised by the relative youthfulness of some parents. Though I ought to know better, I'm always expecting to see people who look like *my* parents. I hear the word "parent," and I picture my retired mother and father. Then this lithesome woman in designer jeans strolls in and says, "Hi, I'm Lisa's mom." "Hey, that's pretty good," I say to myself. "Now who are you, really?" But most of the jolt comes from the recognition of the fact of the parents them-selves—that there are people on the other end of the school bus route who know what I'm assigning, who've heard my jokes, who've read my comments on the backs of composi-tions. Of course I know they're there, just as I know that there's blood in my body. Still, the sight of blood or of parents always seems to come like a revelation.

The unfortunate truth is that parents stand in relation to the classroom as fathers once stood, and in many ways still stand, in relation to the delivery room. It is their job to pace nervously outside, to receive a few progress reports, to wave through the glass, to pay the bill and hand out cigars when the mess is all done. It's tidier that way, better for all con-cerned. Let them in, and the next thing you know they're punching the obstetrician or puking on the floor. Besides, most of them don't really *want* to know more than they have to. The irony, even the tragedy, of the analogy applies as well, in that a process that might serve to strengthen a family only serves to alienate its members. It's no surprise that at the same time as we see a move toward home births, we see a similar move toward home schooling—and not just for the sake of family togetherness. But both are beyond the means of most parents. The challenge schools and teachers need to face is how to make the classroom, like the hospital, more inclusive and thus more humane.

Admittedly, there are obstacles, not the least of which is

a deep-seated and at times well-founded distrust between school and parents. Many parents feel as though all we really want them to do is pay up and shut up. One wonders if they're far off the mark. Education groups calling for "greater parent involvement" seem not so much to be saying that involved parents will mean better-educated students as to be suggesting that if we let parents see more of what we do, they won't mind paying us more to do it. Instead of a revolution in parent-school relations, we call for a better grade of public relations. We don't want parents informed about education so much as we want them converted to its "interests"—as defined, of course, by educators. As I write, there is a school not far from mine whose children's parents have not even been told that the teacher-principal and one of his staff resigned the first week of school, leaving a number of students with substitute instructors. This is "a delicate personnel matter." So let us not be indelicate, but let us also not forget who employs the personnel.

On the other side, teachers and administrators tend to feel, also with some justification, that parents often get involved to the detriment of a school. What Yeats said of our century can sometimes be said of a school community: "The best lack all conviction, while the worst / Are full of passionate intensity"—mostly a parsimonious intensity. When the concern is ideological rather than fiscal, things can go from bad to worse. Not long ago, two parents protested vehemently that the social studies textbooks in a local grade school were biased and inaccurate for stating that the modern state of Israel was founded in 1948 instead of the 13th century B.C.E. and for failing to state that the sole definition of "Palestinian" is "Arab trespasser." This in turn brought a few garbled cries from the peanut gallery to the effect that people who feel that way ought to pack up and move to Israel. (Eventually, the couple did just that—Israel's gain, Vermont's loss.) Well, say some, the less of that kind of thing the better. I agree. I think the students agree. I think that sometimes we teachers get a fair measure of impunity simply because our students prefer to endure almost anything other than the embarrassment of a parental "advocate."

Nevertheless, I think the corrective lies in greater parental involvement, not less. The more who become involved, the less damage any single minority can do to the curriculum. And the more parents become involved in the educational process, as compared merely to being told about it, the more valuable that process becomes as a power for good. We know all about how parents can ban books; we talk very little about how books might enlighten parents. I sometimes think that in a community such as ours, where so many kids miss school in order to work in the barn or provide child care, we might serve them best not by a stricter policy on truancy, but by *requiring* them to spend certain days in the barn and the day-care center while *requiring* their parents to attend a certain number of in-school seminars on such topics as the Plight of the Palestinians, the History of Anti-Semitism, and the Seven Billion Wonders of the World. Break the mill windows with a dictionary; drive a tractor through the library wall.

Many teachers, even many parents, would say that the major obstacle to improved relations between parents and school is not mutual distrust so much as parental apathy. Parents talk wasteful budget, aloof administration, and "nobody tells us nothing," but what it all boils down to is that they plain don't care. School is a baby-sitting service they hate to pay for but wouldn't be without—that's all. Even those of us who can't accept this premise as a major one have to admit that in at least a few cases it is true. One thing that teaching has taught me in a way I can never ignore is that there is no inherent sanctity in parenthood, just a number of parents who are probably saints. After my daughter was born, I came into my classes and said, "This exprience has shown me something I needed to see, and now when I look at my

Sarah, I think also of you, and what I think is that every one of you is someone's Sarah. Every one of you is precious in a way I hadn't thought much about before." That's a lovely sentiment and a good hypothesis on which to base one's treatment of one's students, but as a statement of fact it's a load of bull. It was a stupid thing to say, and it could only have served to depress some of my students. What do I know about their parents, or anyone else's? I am a typical middle-class parent of my generation: I had all kinds of fun, I entertained all kinds of misgivings for over a decade, and then with enough money to aid me, enough experience to guide me, and enough gray hairs to realize that money and experience alike go to the worms, I became a father at thirty-one. I became a father by way of "conversion," and doubtless speak with a convert's tiresome enthusiasm about the joys of learning catechisms that to someone raised in the religion were but the waste of a sunny Saturday morning.

My experience of parenthood is not the same as that of a man whose children only serve to remind him how poor he is, how young he once was, how easy it is when one is young to fall in love with a pretty smile, how quickly a smile loses its constancy and its teeth, and how hard it is to fix teeth or destiny when you're raising four kids on eleven thousand dollars a year. That's not to correlate love of one's children with age or class—I don't even need to spend an example illustrating the fallacy of *any* correlation of *any* material factor with a parent's love. It's only to say that a parent's love for or interest in children is a gift, not a given. I remember a girl writing about "communication problems" with her father. "I'm sure your father loves you," I said, and I wasn't simply mouthing a platitude. I knew her father, and to hear him talk I had to believe that he cared for his children if any man did. I should have realized that he talked too much. "I'm sure your father loves you"—how bitterly ironic that must have sounded, how utterly idiotic I must have looked to that

poor girl who, it now seems pretty certain, was sexually in-
itiated like all of her sisters before her by that ever-loving
father. "I'm sorry I didn't come to your Confirmation," a
girl's alcoholic father writes on a greeting card, "but your
mother is an asshole." And your teacher is one too, if he
claims to be sure about anything concerning your dad—including his being a lost cause.

But granting all that I dare not assume, I still believe it is
neither apathy nor distrust, nor even the two together, that
keeps so many parents away, that makes some back-to-school
nights so desolate. What I'm about to say will probably sound
alien to teachers in affluent communities, where back-to-school
nights should be called "opening nights," and crowds of well-
dressed parents come with their busy questions, pet theories,
favorite authors, and a list of ninety-five learning disabilities
which explain why a surgeon's son does not get but ought
to get straight A's, and which the surgeon will cheerfully nail
to your head if there's no room on the door. "They think of
me as a waiter," says a friend teaching in such a community.
"They pay good money for the food, and I'm there to give
prompt, respectful service." I don't think any of my students'
parents think of me as a waiter. I think some of them probably
see being a waiter as a pretty glamorous job. And I think
they see school as a pretty intimidating place. For many, it
was a stage for failure, bewilderment, and shame. Now they
come back to face a teacher—are they also surprised by how
young he is?—and for some that is like facing a judge. Do
they half-consciously expect me to hold a gavel, to ask why
their homework isn't done, to impose a stiff penance? "I
wasn't ever good in school. If I'd a finished, maybe I could
help her with her homework more. Her mother and I are
separated, divorced actually. She's a hard girl to handle sometimes. I'm working two jobs . . ." It is a parent facing the
grim, bespectacled reaper and saying, "Take me instead. I
was a failure before my daughter was." No wonder so many

stay home! What must it be like when the parents are worse off than most I meet, and the child's problems more serious? My wife, a special educator in the school district, ponders how it must feel to have a kid that neighbors call "not right" and to sit in your broken trailer as a team of college-educated, aerobically exercised young women come one after the other, like inquisitive magi, bearing what you can only hope are gifts of help, promise, and absolution.

I think that one of the challenges faced by a rural teacher, or an inner-city teacher, is how to give kids a sense of the value of an education without devaluing their uneducated parents. Certainly there are cases where the balance is almost impossible to strike, tempting not to bother to strike. The year before I started teaching, a mother wrote in to announce that her son was dropping out: "At least he'll be working at something useful instead of sitting on his ass behind a book." A man at the annual budget meeting rose and shouted, "If I had my way, this place here wouldn't even exist. All any of 'em does anyways is smoke dope and chase girls." But these are extreme and unusual cases—they hardly nullify the problem. Recently I was struck by a passage in Ernest Hebert's *The Dogs of March,* in which a young man in northern New Hampshire scrutinizes his mill worker father:

> He could be counted on to wear forest-green work suit, white t-shirt, red and white suspenders, scuffed shoes or work boots, and white cotton socks, and always the buttons buttoned on his breast pockets, although this meant buttoning and rebuttoning the cigarette pocket twenty times a day. Difficult to tell whether the habit was an expression of personal pride or a Pavlovian trick played on him by the army.
>
> Freddy began now to read his book. He felt more kinship toward Camus' characters than toward his family.

And we know who gave Freddy the book and the knowledge of Pavlov. When I first read that description, I thought, That is how I'm going to dress for work from now on. But that's a little too precious, and I was not taught to teach by wearing clothes. A better method is to instill in students a sense of the gains to be had by sitting on one's ass behind a book, *and* to have them read books like *The Dogs of March,* and the stories of Howard Frank Mosher, Tillie Olsen, and Steinbeck, always Steinbeck. When I was in high school, the kids who read literature outside of class read Salinger and Hesse; here they often read a few more books by Steinbeck, and we know why. And if we can have them read with their parents, or aloud to their parents, and then invite the parents in to tell us what the critics could never know—then we will have taken an important step, and made some important friends.

Before they started Steinbeck, though, I'd have the parents read some of what their own children write. "Do you show this to your parents?" I ask. "Well, sometimes, yeah, once in a while." "Show them!" For if the parents saw much of what I read about parents, they might be amazed at how much they count, and the school might have made another contribution to increased parent involvement. Parents are often led to believe that they have the same value in a teenager's life as does a broken shell on a hatched chick's head. With any luck, it'll drop off, and life will go on. From my desk, the matter looks different. "Name a public figure you respect," I ask on a list of questions designed to help kids think of research topics. A girl answers: "My mother." Surely this has something to say either about how carelessly kids read questions or about how easily one can become a public figure in Albany, Vermont. But most of what is said by the answer is revealed in the girl's response to a subsequent question. "After whom would you model your life?" Again she answers "My mother." The answers are noteworthy, not exceptional.

In the study of literature, too, kids often show a greater interest in parent characters than in those with whom we expect them to identify. Odysseus' yearning for his son is for my students no less poignant or important that Telemakhos' yearning for a father. They'd rather see Odysseus and Penelope reunited than see Telemakhos get a girlfriend. While keeping an anxious and appreciative eye on their children, parents often fail to see their children keeping a not dissimilar eye on them. Not long ago, my wife and I bought a book called *Once Upon a Potty* to read to our daughter, then in toilet training. The last illustration shows the protagonist, little Prudence, sitting contentedly on the chamber pot whose use she has finally mastered. The focus of the page and of the parent who reads it aloud to the toddler is supposed to be on the little girl's admirable achievement. But what *my* little girl wants to know is "Where'd the mommy go?" That long-suffering character is missing from the picture, and it takes some effort on my part to convince our daughter that using a toilet does not cause one's mother to disappear.

It will also take some effort to convince our schools and communities that learning to read Spanish or program a computer need not cause one's mother to disappear, either.

Now that I am a novice father, back-to-school nights have a greater spirit of mutuality about them. I can commiserate a little more with my students' parents, and they can advise me about my child as I sometimes advise them about theirs. We compare experiences; I enjoy this. Often they'll say to me, "Wait till she's a teenager." When people used to say, "Wait till you have kids of your own," I never gave the words much thought; having kids seemed remote enough, or having people assume I'd have kids seemed presumptuous enough to prevent much else from sinking in. Now what they say sounds very real, and foreboding. I may lack firsthand experience of what prompts a teenager's parent to say, "Wait," but I'm close enough to the subject to ponder it with imagination. And it may be that I have seen difficulties in raising a teenager that even a teenager's parent fails to grasp fully. Short of nuclear holocaust or turning into a teenager myself with the approach of midlife senility, nothing terrifes me so much as what another decade will bring to my home, will do to my daughter. Yet one sees so many good kids, so many admirable parents—surely there's reason to hope.

Last spring my student Eddie came to me with what looked ominously like the start of wrinkles at age fifteen. He thought his marking period grade was lower than he deserved. Very respectfully, he told me that he'd averaged his grades and come to a higher figure; just as respectfully, I told him that his math was probably better than mine, and we worked it out together. My math was all right, but I had included a score which Eddie claimed he had earned the right to waive; he'd taken the test and gotten the waiver from my department head, who teaches several units in my class as part of a team-teaching arrangement. I was a little slow in checking the particulars with her. A new marking period was beginning; I was absorbed in concerns that seemed more important. Again with considerable tact, Eddie urged me to get moving, if I "could find the time," because as it stood, his grade was a C, and his mother had told him, "Anything less than a B, and you don't play baseball." Even with the waiver, his grade looked like a C+, but Eddie felt that a slight improvement would make the baseball issue more negotiable.

My department head and I finally got together with our grade books. Her recollection of the test in question was unclear, but she said, "If Eddie says that's the agreement we made, go with it. He's an honest young man, and he's never been a complainer." Apparently Eddie was as lucky to have had her for a teacher as I am to have her for a boss.

Since I'd kept Eddie waiting too long already, I stopped by his house after school with the news. I beat him home, so I chatted for a few minutes with his father, a soft-spoken, muscular farmer with a French accent. His immaculate farm crowned the hill with freshly painted barn and house, both roofed with glinting metal. Black-and-white cows dotted the green pastures—what green pastures! In northeastern Vermont we are snowed under for so long that when the green finally comes in its dozen springtime shades, it just about hurts, the way the sun hurts eyes that have spent the afternoon in a movie theater. The high school was visible in the distance. I wondered how it felt to do chores in sight of one's school, and if the noise of baseball games could be heard out here. Eddie and his mom pulled into the yard.

The four of us stood talking between the house and barn. Eddie had been right about the test. His grade was indeed a very high C, a healthy C, a robust C, a C about to turn into a B. His mother was unimpressed. "Eddie is capable of an A," she said. I agreed; she was right. Nevertheless, I went on, it had been a tough marking period and Eddie had done some impressive work. And it was possible—though this might not make a difference as far as the baseball went, and it was certainly the parents' place to decide that—it was possible I could give Eddie a "point loan." He could take what he needed to make his mark a B, and pay up at the end of the next marking period. I wasn't giving anything away; we'd just make the letters look better. I didn't do this all the time— one point added to a whole average is like five points added to half a dozen tests—but I had done so several times in the past, and I would have no qualms doing so for someone like Eddie. "As Miss Underwood says, Eddie is an honest young man and he's never been a complainer."

It was then that I noticed the father's face—that I looked at it intently for the first time. There are instances where a whole complex of emotions is written on a face; the lips part just so and a ten-thousand-word ticker tape rolls out between them. We read it in the time it takes to nod our heads once.

My Eddie *is* an honest young man, that's a fact. He works hard, at least on the farm. His mother says he could work harder at school, and she is probably right. But it is a hard thing to say to a boy, You cannot play baseball. It is hard on us, hard on him. I think maybe we are too hard—then I think we are too easy. There is no way to know. Working is simple, desire is simple—but having a boy to raise, it is not so simple. It is not enough to labor with all your strength, it is not enough to surrender to your feelings, or even to control your feelings. One of Eddie's teachers told his class that the Persians of long ago would think about a problem drunk, and then think about it sober, but a parent has to think always drunk and sober at the same time, wild and hung over all at once, to figure out how to give a kid the love he needs and whatever else he will need—because love is not enough to make it in a world where people tell jokes about the stupid Frenchmen and a bank can come and take away a farm, or an English teacher or mother and father or all three of them can take a baseball mitt out of a boy's hand when he is young and it is spring like it won't come spring ever again because soon the snow falls and he is too old and has too much work to do to play ball. I don't know what we will do. But I know you and this Miss Underwood are right, sir, when you say our Eddie is no complainer. And when you look at me, you know that, too, though I could cry now because you have said it.

When I leave school the next day, Eddie is leaving too— dressed in a baseball uniform. He grins at me on his jog to the practice field. He is truly a fine young man, but no less young than he is fine, and he will need to grow some before he fully understands who performed the most heroically in the quiet little drama that took place outside his barn. Later in a composition written during his fourth and strongest marking period, he will speak of two people he respects a great deal: Larry Bird and Mr. Keizer. The extravagance of the comparison is almost greater than I can comprehend. Larry Bird! I would have been more than content with Abraham Lincoln.

Skylla and Kharybdis

And all this time,
in travail, sobbing, gaining on the current,
we rowed into the strait—Skylla to port
and on the starboard beam Kharybdis, dire
gorge of salt sea tide.

—*The Odyssey*

*I*f I were to ask one of my students or one of my students' parents to write a philosophy of education, I think I know where he or she would start. As a teacher, I try to start at the same place, for when we lose sight of the expectations of our students and their community, we have for all practical purposes lost the means for achieving our own ideals.

My student or my student's parent would most likely speak of school as a preparation. It gets one ready for life; it makes one fit for the "real world." More specifically, it is the prerequisite for a good job. Those who already have a good job, those who got the good preparation and who come from backgrounds where good jobs and good preparations are the rule, can afford to point out all the shortcomings of such a view. I myself will shortly attempt to point out what I see to be the shortcomings of such a view. But I would never belittle or oppose it—especially not here, in rural Vermont, where so much good faith rests on the promise of school to provide a better economic life. "Back to basics" may be the hackneyed

67

phrase of a few politicians, but it is also the cry of working parents who have struggled for the material basics all their lives, and who see in educational basics the hope for giving their children something better. It is a cry we need to hear.

In an English class the basics that prepare a student for the world include a competence in written and spoken expression, the ability to select topics and to organize and revise material through successive drafts, a working knowledge of English grammar and usage, an enriched vocabulary and the skills to gain and apply it, a broad understanding of literary genres and the principles of literary interpretation, effective strategies for reading, test-taking, and research—all these with numerous details as revised according to what has worked and what has not. When I see a former student, my third question after "How are you?" and "What are you doing these days?" is "How well did we get you ready—what should we have taught you?"

I listen hard to the answers. But I listen knowing that the nineteen-year-old in college or in the army, on the job or on the dole, does not have *all* the answers. Neither do the recruiters, personnel officers, and deans who never tire of telling us what we ought to be teaching. A sad thing happens when the "real world's" self-appointed spokespersons are allowed to dictate curriculum. It is possible to get so far "back to basics" that we lose the most basic things of all. We avoid the monster Skylla only to sail into the whirlpool of Kharybdis.

For consider, if the real world is as full of injustice, waste, and woe as it appears to be, and school has no other purpose than to prepare young people to man and woman the machinery of the real world, then schools are pernicious institutions. They serve to perpetuate rather than remedy evils. We would do as well to burn as to maintain a school that does no more than mirror and foreshadow the real world. And I think no school, even the worst school, does only that.

As I write, two boys have been called to the principal's office for buying the apple cider pressed by the Future Farmers of America and selling it to gullible teachers at a dollar over the F.F.A. price. I assume they will be reprimanded. Apparently our principal does not entirely hold with the values of the real world. If he did, he'd give the boys a kind of testimonial similar to the ones awarded salesmen who understand that schoolteachers often can't recognize a painted-over jalopy any better than they can an overpriced gallon of cider. At the very least, the principal might rebuke the boys for not using their own label or for failing to justify thievery in the name of supply and demand. But our principal, realist though he may be, is an uncompromising utopian in this case. These boys are in trouble. And for that our society can be thankful.

A truly effective school is always both realistic and utopian. It prepares students to survive the real world, and it prepares them to make a more humane world. The latter preparation without the former is that Summerhill kind of experiment which makes exquisite little tragedies out of its students. The former without the latter makes a tragedy of a civilization— the kind we see unfolding all around us, where men and women have ample means to buy the latest toys, but scant means to wrestle with new ideas. In how many households aren't children told to turn off the TV, not because the TV is interfering with the life of the mind, but because a premature obsession with TV might ultimately stunt one's earning power, and hence the ability to buy a TV of one's own someday.

Many decisions we make in a classroom have to do with the Kharybdis-Skylla tension between the demands of the real world and the possibility of a better one. The use of cooperative learning projects is an example. Usually they are justified—too apologetically, I think—in the name of the real world. We say that it's good to have kids work together in groups because they'll need to do the same on the job. Rarely do we say that cooperative learning might be a step toward changing the character of our society, or that it might be a way to teach kids about a fundamental human need. There's a good deal of talk these days about the lure of "cults"—no less in this area, where the Northeast Kingdom Community Church in Island Pond has drawn media attention and converts from across the country. I have sometimes thought that a few cooperative learning projects do more to address the problem than scores of investigative reporters and pompous psychologists. "The lure of cults" is quite often no more than the thrill of solidarity discovered for the first time and mistaken for a miracle. It is not the result of brainwashing any more than our fathers' nostalgia for their service days comes of senility or warmongering. In pup tents and ashrams people have found what a classroom not overly slavish about its allegiance to the job market might also show them: that one of the great joys of human life is working with a goal higher than that of beating out the next guy. I fantasize about a disciple of some totalitarian religion one day approaching a student of ours and saying, "It's great where we are. We're working together, looking out for each other, thinking of something more than just ourselves." "Yeah, I know about that," says the student. "They made us take it in high school."

I suppose I'm saying that by refusing to take the "real world" too seriously or too literally we may actually do a better job of preparing kids for it. I have a boy in one of my classes who is obsessed with snowmobiles. He rides them, repairs them, rebuilds them—and if he had his way, he would write about them every time he had a choice of topic. Almost invariably, I give him his way. In my expository writing class he wrote compositions using illustration, classification, comparison-contrast, analogy, process analysis, and cause-and-effect analysis—all centered on snowmobiles. Now Kharybdis says to me: What happens when he takes his first college composition course out in the real world with an instructor who will find *one* essay on snowmobiles tedious, let alone half a dozen?

Skylla replies: But what if his destiny in the real world is to be a writer about snowmobiles? What if thanks to your indulgence he authors a classic entitled *The Compleat Snowmobiler,* in which urbane winter sportsmen are led by pleasing arguments to give precedence to snowmobiling as the best *and holiest* of cold-weather pursuits? "Gentlemen, I grant most readily that had the Sea of Galilee frozen, the disciples would have labored as ice fishermen; yet in the traversing of the lake and thus in the spreading of the Gospel they would have been snowmobilers, and in no wise cross-country skiers, as some flatlanders falsely boast . . ."

Kharybdis rejoins: You're being silly. And anyway, he is far more likely to become the Izaak Walton of snowmobiles by developing his skills through writing on a variety of subject areas than he is by remaining sequestered in one. Skylla again: By the same token, he is more likely to please a professor or any other reader by a passionate obsession than by a contrived versatility. As long as his compositions are legitimate narrative, exposition, or argument, why shouldn't a teacher allow him to have a legitimate subject, that is, one about which he really has something to say?

I give the point to Skylla, and another approving nod to the snowmobile. A colleague of mine, no less sensitive to the stakes than I, calls it differently and limits the number of snowmobile compositions she'll read. In the area of "book report" assignments, however, she is more tolerant of unorthodox obsessions than I. Of course each of us feels more comfortable about his or her decision knowing that the other has adopted a different one. The possibility of such balance ought to be borne in mind by those in the real world who see rigidly defined curriculums as the way to build the New Jerusalem, or at least the New Tokyo.

The typical English class assignment of keeping a journal

is another instance of the teacher's dilemma of how much to "be not conformed to this world." Probably some would object to journal-keeping on the grounds of its having so little application to the job market. Unless one is going to be an author or a ship's captain, what's the point? We'd do better to have kids concentrate more on research writing or even journalism than journals. The same argument can be used against all kinds of "creative" writing, and I hardly need say at this point that I reject it as spurious.

But I also have some strong reservations about journal-keeping, and these, curiously enough, have to do with what I see as a troubling resemblance between the assignment and the ways of the real world. Try as I might to distinguish a journal from a diary, kids see little difference between the two. That failure may simply be the teacher's failure to distinguish an adult's powers of reflection from a teenager's, and to make allowances for the difference. In any case, assign a journal and one ends up reading a diary; and here it is that I find myself preparing my students, against my will, for the real world. For we live in a culture that puts a high value on self-revelation, an inordinately high value, I think. We attend what purports to be a lecture on dinosaurs only to hear about a paleontologist's relationship with his mother. Someone seated behind us whispers, "This is so much better than I expected!" What were you expecting, *Oedipus the King?* By having my students keep journals, and by unwittingly tempting them to interest me at the cost of self-disclosure, am I not teaching them to pimp their privacy for the all-too-curious real world?

The problem is compounded when I find myself inadvertently descending from editor to advice columnist. A girl writes in her journal: "What do you do with a boyfriend who's only interested in *your top?*" Between the puritan in me that would say, "Please don't ask me that," and the cynic that would say, "The top may lead to less trouble than the bottom," the paternal English teacher writes: "I'd be sure to remember that I was more than a 'top' and I'd insist that others remember the same thing"—all very sweet, sincere, and well intentioned, but all pretty creepy too—another case, perhaps a prototypical case, of the troubled female opening her heart to the man of heart, and diploma, and tie, a situation with which our culture is already sick unto death. This just isn't what I had in mind. I have yet to give a journal assignment without vowing never to do so again.

But I always break my vow, for several reasons. First, the kids like journals, and whereas pleasure cannot be the sole determiner of what we do in school, it is still an important one. Second, journals get otherwise taciturn kids to write. Third, though it may carry the risk of excessive self-disclosure, a journal can teach self-reflection, an ability that may not help one get a job but may help one keep some sanity once a job's been gotten. And finally, there are times in the real world when kids have real problems and few chances to confide in someone about them. Journals have allowed me to intervene effectively, if not quite comfortably, in a few instances. Just don't feel you have to spill your guts to get an A, I tell the class. Remember the difference between a journal and a diary. Review movies. Write scurrilous songs. Lie. You don't *have* to *tell* me anything—an instruction which invariably leads someone to conclude that I can be trusted with everything.

The examples so far have to do with relatively minor decisions worthy of an individual teacher's consideration, but hardly weighty matters of curriculum. There is a matter, however, on which the real world and any school that resists taking its claims as absolute are going to clash. One does not have to be a prophet to know that the clash will occur over computers.

Only an idiot will deny that we are in the midst of a computer revolution, that its effects will be far-reaching, and that schools are in the vanguard of the movement. Naturally enough, a few stubborn "humanists" are going to resist the changes, seeing in them a challenge to the superiority of "the arts" and to the right of old dogs to forgo new tricks, especially when those tricks have to do with gadgetry. By disposition, I'm an old dog myself, but I see plainly enough that all of this is pride and fear and sloth, and needs to be swept away as such.

What I also see, however, and what I am not sure so many others see, is that computers have the potential to swallow our curriculums whole and to turn our educational system into little more than a tax-supported trade school for high-tech industries and their products. I fear that our preoccupation with artificial intelligence is becoming a form of the same. I hear a pervasive dogma that says anything done on a computer is better than anything done any other way—not because the computer is necessarily more efficient but because the computer is, well, a computer, and after all, this is the age of computers. I have a new program that enables my computer to put on a pair of pajamas, and to think that for all those years I went to the bother of wearing them myself. I have a computer that permits a three-year-old child to draw pictures, and to think of all the time we wasted and mess we made using crayons, watercolors, and finger paints. No, I cannot help you now because I am learning to use this computer, which will enable me to help you even more by saving me time, just like all those other timesaving devices which have made my life so complex and debt-ridden that I need a "personal" computer to keep track of it.

Somewhere someone needs to ask, "What, exactly, are we doing here? Who, exactly, is the beneficiary? What, precisely, is the difference, not only between a human mind and a computer, but also between a human being and a sheep?" If the questions do not arise in education, I fear they will not arise at all.

Neither I nor my school is going to ask them. We in the

Northeast Kingdom are breathless enough from trying to catch up with that part of the computer revolution which is very real and very present without taking time to question the next step. In those parts of the real world where reality is hard and resources are few, when IBM talks, people listen. Among my students, I probably sound more like another evangelist for the microchip than like a teacher with misgivings. As far as I'm concerned, those misgivings are my private luxury, like a volume of erotic or devotional poetry that one reads but refrains from sharing with minors. Yet I do try to give my students the means whereby they might one day ask the critical questions.

Occasionally I tease them by asking why they think we're bothering to learn this or that. "So we can pass your course," they'll answer almost at once.

"But why pass my course?" I ask.

"Because we'll need it for college," the more serious will say.

"Ah, but what do you need college for?"

"To get a good job."

"And the good job, why do you need that?"

At this point someone tires of the game and blurts out, "To live! You need a job to live!"

"But why do you need to live? In other words, after you have read the book for the grade, after you have the grade for the course, and the diploma for the job, and the job for the living, and a car and a videocassette recorder and a computer that organizes your sock drawer—then what? Where do you go from there? What is your *purpose* then?" It is a question they would do well to ask who maintain in the hoary name of relevance that vocational kids need only know how to swing a hammer and write a business letter, so why trouble them with poetry?

My favorite reply to this was written by a man who felt he had too little time for poetry. In the day of our country's founding, John Adams wrote: "I must study politics and war, that my sons may have liberty to study mathematics and philosophy . . . [and] commerce and agriculture, in order to give their children a right to study painting, poetry, [and] music." There is some reason to be nostalgic over men and women such as this.

But what would poor John Adams say to the rightful heir of his vision who claims that he must study poetry so he can pass English and "get a good job with computers"? I know what I would say. I would say that perhaps this student has apprehended a new kind of poetry of which Mr. Adams was ignorant. I say let us give this person all he needs to get the job he wants, and let us do our job so well that it will seem to him as though we read the printout of his future and planned our lessons accordingly. But let us read the *whole* printout. Let us perceive that in addition to data processing he must have some grasp of life's complexity, and of his own mortality. Let us give him some means to fill that void which cannot be filled simply by cluttering a screen with graphics, or by blacking in an oval with a number-two lead pencil.

Criticism and Wonder

Downriver a loon hooted. Its long wild call floated over the water and trees and snow as I stood with empty arms on the edge of my youth in a place wheeling sunward, full of terror, full of wonder.

—HOWARD FRANK MOSHER, *Disappearances*

An unexamined life is not worth living.

—SOCRATES

Sometimes as a way of introducing mythology, and of illustrating why it is not accurate to think of myth as naive science, I tell my classes how I came to know the facts of life. Young people listen carefully to a talk like that. There's the rare chance they may be missing a fact or two.

One evening just after sunset, I begin, I was sitting in the back seat of a 1955 Chevrolet (full attention from audience— How old was Keizer in '55?—Who else was alive back then?— Did they do it in cars?) parked at the Paterson General Hospital in New Jersey. My father and my grandmother were in the front seat. I was three years old. (Audience relaxes—this'll be a long one.) We were there because my mother was inside having my brother, Henry, though at the time, of course, I didn't know that the baby was going to be a brother or that it'd be named Henry if it was. I did know that a baby was on its way, and I asked my father, as I'm sure that all of you have by this time asked your parents: Where do babies come from?

My father, who probably didn't need to be answering such questions at that particular time, told me that the angels bring the babies down from heaven.

Wise guy in back: "You mean they don't?"

"Well, stay tuned and you'll find out."

I'm not sure to what extent I'm remembering that moment accurately, and to what extent it's been colored by the dreams I've had since and by the mind's tendency to revise memories, but when I recall my father's answer I am turning to look out the car window at the black skyline of the city, and there are still just a few red streaks from the sunset, and I imagine the angels my father has just told me about. They're giants. They stand on the city. All I can see are their legs; the tops of their thighs are lost in the clouds. Maybe because it is evening, or maybe because we are in a city where there are many dark-skinned people, the angel legs are all black. And I hear singing—a choir of deep voices singing one note, something like "au," very strong and sonorous. Suddenly, two long black arms come out of the sky, and cradled in their massive hands, swinging gently, lower and lower over Paterson, New Jersey, is a little white baby, our baby.

As time went on, I had some questions for my father: Why did the angels bring babies to hospitals? Wouldn't home be more convenient or church more appropriate? Why did only mothers "have them"? What's a womb? Things of that nature. My father then told me that babies grow from an egg inside a mother's stomach, which seemed a lot less credible than what he had told me before, except that it fitted the facts as I knew them, so I accepted it. But soon there were other problems. For instance, if the baby comes from the mother, why do fathers say that children are their own flesh and blood? Wouldn't they only be a mother's flesh and blood? So my father told me that the man gives the woman a seed from his body to add to her egg and together they form a baby. This answer raised its own set of concerns, namely the precise source of the seed, and my growing fear that it was removed from some place on a man's body by means of an unspeakably dreadful operation, which explained why men were often seen standing around at gas stations and barber-shops looking grim. Finally, my questions became too numerous, and my father told me the full story of where babies come from, which given my age and the times in which I grew up, was surprisingly candid and complete.

I was told two versions of the facts of life, one involving angels and one involving seeds and eggs. Two years ago my wife gave birth to our daughter, and I was finally able to figure out which version is true.

I pause to let the class laugh.

Then I say: They both are. I know the second version is true because my wife and I did that thing my father had described, and sure enough, we made a baby. But I also know the original story is no less true, for when I saw the terrific force of my wife's pushing, when the doctor told me I could cut the cord that joined mother and daughter, when a new mouth cried out and a new pair of eyes looked into mine, I was surrounded by something large and dark and soulful and singing, and I can only call it angels because I have no other words.

In class, the point of my story is that there are different ways of making sense out of phenomena, that a technical explanation may not be the same thing as a full account, and that in their seemingly fanciful stories the ancient Africans, Celts, Greeks, Hebrews, Hindus, and Sumerians may not even be *trying* to ask "How does it work?" so much as "What does it mean?"

Here in this essay, the point of my story has to do with two abilities within the human mind, both present from child-hood: the ability to be critical and the ability to feel wonder, the ability to doubt and the ability to marvel, the drive to seize the facts of life from out of an awesome obscurity and the tendency to be awed once the facts are known—to ask "why" and to exclaim "ah." With one faculty and not the other we are either machines or savages, droids or druids.

If there are two great commandments for shaping the mind of a student, they are surely akin to these: Thou shalt instruct criticism; thou shalt instill wonder. I do not think their application is confined to only one subject area, or to that group of subject areas we have smugly named the humanities. Mathematics, for example, is a means for criticizing anything from a restaurant check to a political promise; it is also a marvel of the human mind and of nature, so much so that philosophers cannot agree on which realm's numbers are the most marvelous. Coaching football is both critiquing an incompleted pass and taking off one's hat for lack of knowing what else to do when a kid goes fifty yards for a touchdown. To teach and to learn are to criticize and to wonder.

It may be that we teachers hesitate to give these faculties their full due. Wonder seems either useless, or else "natural" enough to require no deliberate stimulation. For criticism we can think of some specific uses, but aren't kids critical enough? Occasionally a colleague will say to me, "Do you have Philip for anything? Do you notice how he's got to challenge everything you say?"

"Yes," I'll answer. "I've been encouraging him to do that."

But I'm also keeping an eye on Phil. The virtues we teach kids are quickly turned to vices. Teach the uses of a semicolon, and commas become an endangered species. Encourage a kid to be critical, and he or she is likely to be no more than difficult. Has Philip concluded that a Socratic gadfly is no more or less than a pain in the neck? If so, the corrective lies in greater critical acumen, not less. Even our critical skills need to be disciplined by a set of critical perspectives. Otherwise our search for clarity and our insistence on honesty become little more than clever means for dodging whatever makes a demand on us. Certainly kids are prone to this weakness. Tell them life is utterly absurd and they'll ask you no more than how to spell "absurd." Tell them to look "absurd" up in the dictionary, and they'll engage you in an hour of dialectic just to have the spelling for free.

But teachers and other adults are no less prone to the same weakness. Our dodges are simply more clever, less likely to be detected. For example: How does an English teacher refute a challenge to his social conscience? By criticizing the muckraker's prose. That is merely the complement of a kid's refusal to revise his prose because revisions of that kind are trivial in comparison to the muckraker's findings—as if by butchering a language we could feed our fellow man. Teacher and student, old and young—all of us have been the most stubborn and defensive by pretending to be the most probing and insightful. Perhaps we can help kids see the difference between critical questioning and artful dodging by turning the hard questions on ourselves. Intellectual honesty, like charity, begins at home.

It is tempting to introduce kids to a critical attitude by prodding them to question the popular culture, which they can swallow so uncritically. I know that I have succumbed to that temptation too often. It is a powerful one. Where this side of the emperor Caligula is one going to find targets as inviting as MTV and the latest *Rambo* movie? We still do better, I think, to start closer to home.

The ancient Greeks provide me with a good place in which to begin. My freshmen read Sophocles, Homer, and the myths; I do Aeschylus with the Advanced Placement class. The students know that I admire the Greeks, that I'd rather read *The Odyssey* than almost anything, that I hope to see Athens, that I would have liked to meet Plato. I hope some of the literature as well as some of my appreciation goes out into the world with them. Most of the kids will remember that

Antigone buried her dead brother, that Odysseus had a dog, that Sappho lived on the island of Lesbos. But none of them will leave my class with the impression that the Greeks were a race of gods. Studying them carefully, and critically, leads us to ask questions about their darker side.

One such question that I have never been able to answer satisfactorily for my students or for myself is this: Was Helen of Troy an unfaithful wife or a victim of rape? Aeschylus has Agamemnon say that he raped Troy as a punishment for the rape of Helen. Yet Homer treats her as a woman whose head was turned by a handsome prince. One answer, of course, is that we're dealing with different strands of tradition and different authors' selections from that tradition. But perhaps a better if more troubling answer is that the Greeks never bothered to ask the question. Adultery vs. rape is an issue of will, and Helen's will is scarcely an issue at all. More important for the Greeks are a warrior's honor and a man's rights. To the extent that Helen does have a will, it is swayed by the wills of men. "Force them and they love," writes Lattimore of the presentation of such characters as Helen, Cassandra, and Briseis. So along with beautiful myths that never die, the Greeks contributed to a myth that dies hard— that women want to be raped.

And in this way a teacher proceeds, critical of his or her favorites, critical even of those criticisms. One judges; then one looks hard at one's judgments. We have a tendency, for example, to refute anthropological chauvinism only to indulge in a historical kind. We act like imperialists on the time line instead of on the map. If someone in twentieth-century El Dorado eats his mother for lunch, we urge students to be "nonjudgmental"; if someone in fifth-century Athens called his mother-in-law a battle-ax, he's a pig whose every thought is sullied and suspect. That kind of simplemindedness is surely not confined to high school teachers, but we often get the rap for it. Without the faith in ourselves to question what we have been taught, and the nerve to let the gradebooks slide once in a while so that we can attend to other books, we become the repositories of all kinds of half-truths and bunk: that the Attic tragedians wrote plays to please Aristotle, that art made the Renaissance without any help from usury, that Einstein knew physics and nothing else, that Poe was the Ozzy Osbourne of the nineteenth century, that the struggle for black civil rights began in the early sixties, American radicalism in the late sixties, feminism in the seventies, and insight in the eighties or whenever I first happened to use the word "insight."

Perhaps a high school teacher's greatest piece of potential misinformation is that he or she is something other than a high school teacher, one who teaches students aged fourteen to eighteen. Sparing students half-truths does not mean telling them every truth that occurs to us. It is their minds, not their condition, that our teaching ought to make critical. We need to know when to lighten up. The only line of graffiti I ever read about myself in school was penciled on a desk in my classroom: "Mr. Keizer is a professor." At first I was flattered. To say the least, it seemed a lot more favorable than "Keizer licks wet donkey dinks" or something like that. Lately, though, I wonder if it was.

"Look the next time you bite into a tomato," I tell my writing students, "and realize that in one fruit on one vine there are enough seeds to replant the entire garden. And the vines are loaded with fruit! Nature always makes more than enough so that in the end it will have just enough. That is how a writer takes notes for a composition—with abundance." That is how one takes a tomato, or a dairy cow or a sugar maple, and turns it into a teacher—by opening one's eyes and the eyes of one's pupils to its wonders.

To lead students to wonder is to lead them to the reason that prompted us and countless men and women before us to study those things we teach. At the root of our becoming biology teachers or industrial arts teachers is likely to be our first sight of a nautilus shell or a rolltop desk, wondrously made. I love *The Odyssey*, I tell my students, for its elemental wonder, for its amazement at things, at a two-handled drinking cup crafted by a god or a god-inspired smith, at a bed of leaves that a man heaps over himself, smiling for joy that he will not freeze to death in the night. It was the meeting of Homer's wonder and my own that led me to study the book as well as read it. And if wonder is the seed of our learning, it is just as often the fruit as well. We learn because we wondered, and we learn in order to wonder in ways large enough and varied enough to suit the creatures we are.

I like to make my students wonder. I like to tell them the story of Diogenes, who when asked by Alexander the Great to name whatever favor he desired, told the conqueror to move aside—he was blocking the sun. I like to tell them how Sophocles avoided a shameful old age as ward to a greedy son by quoting from his latest play as proof of a sound mind, and how a Spartan soldier argued against enslaving the vanquished Athenians by reciting their poetry. I like to pound a desk top with my fist and tell them that what I strike contains more empty space than solid. I like to draw a bucket to represent the age of the earth, a drop to be all of humankind's existence, and then to enlarge that drop and show how long we were living in caves. I like to pass around a fat concordance of Shakespeare or the Bible and tell them about men and women who gave their eyesight and the productive years of their lives to compile what a computer can put together and print in a matter of hours. Of course we sometimes form our wonder into questions, lest class become an edition of *Ripley's Believe It or Not*. What would *you* have asked Alexander to give you? What is true wealth, true purpose? Why did the Greeks think so much of poetry? Why do we think so little of it, yet so much of them? Did the concordance compilers waste their lives? How might subatomic theory influence philosophy or art? If the earth is so old and humankind is so young, what can we say about our ecological responsibility?

Still, I cannot think of the wonder as sugar on the pill— it is one of the pill's essential ingredients. How often teachers are retrained and recertified with additional methods for inducing brain death. Would it not be more to the point to replenish our reservoirs of wonder, to give us back the itch to be in a library, to dig something out of the ground, to tell a story, to find some shy and unoccupied minor with whom we can share our enthusiasms?

It is fortunate that the kids themselves often fill the need. Granted, all teachers know what it's like to pass around a scientific instrument or a portrait only to have the lens come back smudged with potato chip grease or Sir Isaac Newton return with antlers and an exposed penis. But we also know what it's like to hand a student some object tarnished with our own familiarity and to have it come back lustrous. The last recording I played during one period devoted to the "other" music was a Bach organ composition, *Komm, heiliger Geist, Herre Gott.* We were almost out of time, and I told the students they were free to leave with the bell. A handful stayed until the piece was finished. I looked at their faces after switching off the turntable, and I remembered what it had been like to come by accident into a college auditorium unoccupied but for a music student seated behind the organ, and to rush down the aisle when she was finished, saying, "What was that? Who wrote that?" One of my students asked a still more basic question. "How many organs were playing?" he said, as if I would need to write the number in scientific notation. His question made me wonder at my own reply, tempted me to doubt what I knew as surely as I was standing before him.

"One."

"One?"

"One."

I felt like Moses descending Sinai with a brand-new revelation. "Hear, O Israel, the organ of Bach is one."

I had known the feeling before. When my remedial writing students were composing their novella, *Born to Run*, I brought in the typed draft of their first chapter and asked them to proofread it. The three of them huddled together and read, and reread, as though they had never seen their own story. Only after a while did I understand: this was probably the first time in their lives that they had seen one of their own sentences *in print*—not published, just in print, in a form other than their handwriting. They stared like guests at Belshazzar's feast; I grinned like Gutenberg.

In the end, a teacher's store of wonder can never be seriously depleted, because he or she works in proximity to wonder every day. The students themselves are the supreme wonders of the world. Just to sit before or pace around a class taking an essay test, to see the pencils bitten and the feet shifted and the sleeves rolling up, to watch as the most self-conscious young men and women forget themselves and contort their faces into the silliest expressions—to watch that concentration and to guess at its curses and eurekas has to be one of the most wondrous experiences a person can know. Dylan Thomas wrote of "The force that through the green fuse drives the flower." Am I not seeing something akin to the force that first drove the fuse itself out of the mud, that drove amoebas into vertebrates, and reptiles into birds, as I watch a classful of kids develop their ideas through branching trees of trial and error, paragraph by paragraph, species by species, in an hour of mental evolution? A girl pushes the hair back

from her eyes, bends forward, and gills become lungs. A fire
drill sounds—naturally!—and a whole race of dinosaurs per-
ishes in a meteoric cataclysm. I can hear their hisses and
moans as the lights go out and I close the door. We return,
the lights go on, a boy inhales deeply and begins scratching
his paper in earnest for the first time—a new mammal scurries
through the brush. Often during a test I find myself repeating
silently a verse from Habakkuk: "The Lord is in his holy
temple; let all the earth keep silence before him"—always
adding for my own benefit, "Just remember, buddy, you ain't
the Lord."

Neither are the kids—but they can inspire wonder until it
feels like worship. Once when I was leaving work for the day
I met a young man at the door who had stayed after school
to make up a mathematics test. "I feel so stupid," he said.
"I feel so ashamed." "How come?" I asked. I could not
imagine why a student like this one could have any legitimate
reason to be *so* ashamed.

"I got real involved in doing this one problem and I
let . . . things get away from me. I wet my pants."

I looked down at his trousers. He sure had. His math
teacher rushed by us to get her car and drive him home before
anyone saw.

I saw, and I will remember for a long time. We all have
our little regrets, our fuel for self-pity, and one of mine is
that I did not go to an Ivy League college. Like many people
with comparable regrets, I probably flatter myself by imagining I even could have done what I wish I'd done. And
I don't deny the fine teaching I received from some very
accomplished instructors, from men and women whose
names I invoke like those of guardian angels. I only wonder
if with wiser planning and higher striving I might have become one of them, I might have seen "professor" and my
name written in some form besides graffiti, I might have de-

veloped greater capacities for criticism and for wonder. But I never would have met this boy. Where at Yale or Stanford or Princeton, where but in this little high school with its back against the woods would I have met a man or woman devoted enough to algebra to piss his or her pants for it?

Off to College

By the waters of Babylon, there we sat down and wept, when we remembered Zion.

—Psalms

"I am looking out the window of my classroom at a cold sun, bare trees, a small farm, and a three-foot blanket of snow. If you travel some distance in the line of my vision, you will see little else until you come to Island Pond, an old railroad town . . . and beyond that, through more trees and snow, to the Canadian border. Andrea grew up in Albany, beside which Island Pond looks almost urban. From the time she came into my freshman English class she has been conspicuous as a bright, perceptive, independent young woman. Had I gone to Harvard, I'd have a better idea of how she measures up to your standards. But then, had I gone to Harvard, I might not be here.

"Andrea has not traveled to Europe, has not worked in a hospice or hunger project, has not published a poem or built a computer. She has taken some of our most difficult courses, including Advanced Placement English, and has maintained a high academic standing—this while helping to care for the emotionally disturbed and mentally retarded foster children in her single-parent household and while managing as many as three other jobs. I know that one might say that laudable as this is, it does not suffice to make her a Harvard student, and I grant the point. Still, I cannot help but ponder how many Harvard men and women will publish papers this year on the causes of and the solutions to Andrea's predicament. After a time, the papers will be superseded and forgotten, but Andrea's struggle will continue unless some person or institution enables her to make a radical break with her present life . . ."

To whom it may concern: Andrea's struggle continues.

All of the courses I teach at present are designed primarily for college-bound students. I am sure that I say the word "college" more during the course of a semester than some preachers say "heaven" in the course of their careers. College is the motto, the carrot, the bogey, the final authority for much of what we do. At times it seems a ridiculous distortion. If my students all acquire prison records, incurable neuroses, bookless shelves—but high SAT scores—then by the dominant standard I've done a good job.

But I won't carry this line of thinking any further; in front of my students, it scarcely goes this far. Nietzsche said doubt is the luxury of those with faith, and where students have so little faith in their abilities and so sketchy an awareness of higher education, we have little luxury for doubt. I do tell my students that college will not necessarily make them better human beings, that it might not even make them wealthier human beings, that there are some miserable human beings sequestered in colleges, and that there are valuable lessons to be learned outside of them. I also tell my students that coming home to Orleans County with a college degree in order to take up farming or homemaking is not a waste of that degree. But this is all by way of qualifying my main idea, which is that every student who can go to college should go, and anyone who goes should go to the best, most rigorous one possible. If they won't heed the former advice, I ask them if they want to end up like their struggling parents. If they won't heed the latter advice, I ask them, only half fooling, if they want to end up like me.

Convincing students to take an interest in college, especially in a superior college, is often nothing more than convincing them that *they* are interesting. Many do not seem to think that they are. The most successful at convincing them otherwise is often the military recruiter. He comes to school dressed in his impeccable uniform, sits in the guidance office or even the lobby, and talks to all comers. What is perhaps more important, he appears to be *listening* to all comers. I both resent his angling where the fish are so hungry and admire his skill as an angler. He brings glossy brochures and free book covers. "Be all that you can be—in the Army." I wonder what effect it might have on my students' aspirations if other recruiters came to freshman classes with free book covers that said "Yale" and "Smith" and "U.C.L.A." I'm wondering, not holding my breath. To many of our kids, as to kids in other economically disadvantaged areas, the armed services are what the medieval church was to their ancestors—the only institution in which a commoner just might have a chance to become somebody. And I do not discourage my students from exploring military careers. I have no ideological objections per se. Neither do most others. The objectors I meet are usually less conscientious than fashionable. I simply let my students know that I should not like to see them come home as a Torpedo Specialist III who thinks he's an electrical engineer, or as a corpse who thought he was a military advisor. Usually they've given more thought to the second than to the first. I also try to let my students know that someone besides the Army or Navy recruiter might find them interesting.

That task is the most intense when I help students with that part of their college applications which requires them to impress the admissions office with an essay. As an English teacher, I feel that after writing letters of recommendation, help of this kind is the best last thing I have to offer my college candidates. The offer stands for any student in the school. The drafts or notes they bring to me are among the most dismal pieces of writing I read in my job. "This sounds like a high school graduation speech," I say to them. Some are no doubt flattered. They didn't think it was *that* good. Respect for their feelings prevents my being blunter: "Do you really believe you are this dull?"

Dullness is the least point of comparison between the essays and graduation speeches. A stronger comparison is the indictment of the student's education implicit in both. The gowned speaker in June tells us, intentionally or not, about the vision we have given him or her in twelve to thirteen years of schooling. Almost invariably, the "vision" comprises a sense of gratitude, a less developed sense of humor, and a knowledge of elocution—nothing less, and nothing to scoff at, surely, but nothing more. And students who come with the prose parts of their college applications tell me where I have failed as their writing teacher. I have failed to teach what may be the most important of all writing skills: to see the significance of one's own experience. Writing a book about the meaning of teaching in the Northeast Kingdom will ultimately remain a paltry achievement until each of my students can write a memorable essay on the meaning of living here.

We start out, as I did in the letter quoted above, by looking out the window, literally or figuratively, at where we are and at what we have done that others have not done. The kid who has all but managed a farm for a disabled father, and who has always thought of his burden as a deprivation—which, of course, it is—now needs to see how it is also a credential. The kid who has shared a household with numerous half-siblings, and who has hitherto thought of them as no more than competitors, now has to realize that they may have been educators as well. The kid who "never went anywhere" out of sight or sound of the furniture mill, and is now about to compete with kids whose summer vacations are all sails, baguettes, and castles, has to understand that for someone with the right eyes and ears, walking through a mill town can be as instructive as bicycling through Amiens, and if one has such eyes and ears, then imagine what Amiens—or Amherst—will reveal to them. Help the reader of your essay to imagine that; help the reader to see that you lack no sensibility for having lacked some opportunity.

If the beginning of such a conference is disheartening, the end can sometimes warm one's heart. What greater reward for a writing teacher than to have a student say, "I think I'll be OK now. I think you've helped me see all I have to write about"? Perhaps all I've failed to teach is that the lessons of composition class have applications elsewhere. Yet that in itself is a serious failure.

When our kids are finally accepted, financially aided, and packed off to college, there begins a period of nervous waiting for those of us who have helped them go. A Northeast Kingdom teacher in the fall is like a Northeast Kingdom gardener in the spring: we "harden off" the young plants as well as we can, but frost may come any time from now until harvest. I feel especially sorry for the parents. Many have not gone to college, and feel helpless to advise or commiserate. My job knows few moments as poignant as when a mother looks over a cash register at me and says, "Would you call her if I paid for the call? She phones almost every night, she's crying, and I don't know what to say to her. I was never there."

Interestingly enough, when I do call, the major complaint is not the difficulty of courses, the inaccessibility of professors, the ache for home—though all are mentioned and all are implicit in the major complaint—but the noise of the dormitories. That complaint, I am sure, comes from more than a rural kid's quiet background. It has more to do with the shattering of a rural kid's illusions. For years the student has prepared for the awesome step of becoming his or her family's first college student. Parties have been missed for the sake of jobs, and jobs have been lost for the sake of study, only so that a young man or woman can go—to a big party. And not a party, even, not the holiday abandonment that breaks through the mundane—but a ruckus that is itself mundane, blind, constant, and ultimately joyless. I can only comprehend a student's disillusionment by analogy to that of a beginning teacher, who leaves college ready to smite down ignorance with a two-edged sword, and whose first job interview begins "How do you see yourself as a disciplinarian?" and ends "What can you coach?" I spoke with a young woman just last night, who a year ago made the difficult choice between a state college close to her home and her boyfriend, and the state university farther away. "I'd have expected this kind of party atmosphere at Johnson or Lyndon. But I'm at the University of Vermont!" Her naiveté is surpassed only by that of a local couple who thought they could gain their daughter peace and privacy at the same institution by complaining to its administrators. Crazy hicks.

I used to have a relative who said that anybody who believed in socialism should go to the post office and buy a stamp. (Had he grown up close to a Vermont post office, he would have campaigned for Norman Thomas.) Well, anyone who thinks the post office is uncooperative should go to a dean of students and suggest that a college's living arrangements ought to be in keeping with its professed purpose. I always laugh at the criticisms leveled at college officials for their failure to control student unrest during periods commonly called "explosive." They can't even guarantee student rest during periods commonly called the middle of the night.

As with other injustices, relatively minor ones like a noisy dormitory are symptomatic of larger ones. When I was in college, a black coed asked her white neighbor on the floor below to turn down her record player. Time has blurred many details of the ensuing argument, but as I recall it ended with the white girl flat on her back in the doorway. The incident was discussed as a racial issue, which it was, but only to the extent that it was also a class issue. I'd lay odds that neither of the girls was much of a racist. But I'd lay the same odds that the black girl was learning every day what it means to come from an impoverished school, that she had a lot of studying to do that night, that if she flunked out of this college she would be a long time in seeing another, and that she didn't have a stereo. She might have felt at home with some of my students, who go to a college not because it's near to the ski slopes or in a city rank with bars, but because it's the best their money, their abilities, or their confidence in their abilities can get them. And how painful it must be for them to notice that difference between themselves and some of their more privileged fellows.

One of my former students, who comes from a family that was recently forced to sell its farm, managed to attend a university by means of massive student loans and a work-study program. During her first semester, her roommate's car was broken into and robbed of an estimated $500 worth of clothing, cosmetics, athletic equipment, and cash. The girl called her father and informed him that she'd lost $1,000 worth of her things. He promptly sent her a check for that amount. My student got to see it before going off to clean rat cages or whatever she does in order to buy books. No doubt she came home to a brand-new, blasting stereo and a few music-lovin' guys seated on her bed. By the waters of Babylon, we sat down and wept.

Whether this economic inequality manifests itself as snobbery, I do not know, but I suspect it does. A reader might say, "How much snobbery can we be talking about? Where do your students go—Vassar? I'd imagine most of them don't leave Vermont, or at least northern New England." Such a reader is correct as regards my students' choice of schools, but he or she may lack some understanding of snobbery. It is not so often the disdain a person on the tenth rung of a ladder shows to one on the first, as it is the disdain someone on the fifth rung of a ladder shows to one on the third. Not long ago an outstanding basketball coach of some reputation married one of our teachers and came to work at one of our schools. A newspaper in the city where he had formerly worked ran a supercilious feature article on his move to the nether regions. The last sentence read: "Who knows? In a couple of years Coach B——may be a regular hick." And where was the newspaper based? Boston? Chicago? New York? Brattleboro, Vermont. Regular hick, indeed.

Most students who stay within the state come home weekends—especially during the first semester. Even those farther away seem to make it home more often than one might expect. I can only guess what homecoming is like for them. I have lived here a little over seven years, too short a time for nostalgia, but when I return from any place outside the Kingdom, and when I pass over Lowell mountain from the west or into one of the St. Johnsbury exits from the south, I feel as though doors have closed behind me and I am in where it is safe and warm—which is odd, because the blue sky often turns to foreboding gray exactly at those points of passing. It is ridiculous to imply that this cloudy region with its share of crime and more than its share of degraded lives is paradise, or that there are not kids who come home only for their parents' sake, and who are happy to be out again. But for many the relief I feel at coming home must be magnified a hundred times. What must it be like to return from almost unbroken anonymity to a place where nearly everyone you meet knows you, greets you, asks how you're getting on. I too have moved from anonymity to familiarity; I know less of what it's like to go in the other direction, the direction these kids took when they went away to college.

My culture shock was learning to trust what they are now

learning to do without. My car goes into a snowbank, and for one shaken moment I feel like a runaway slave as farmers race toward me with a long chain and barking hounds. Behind them comes the tractor to pull me out. I'm on the loading dock of a furniture factory scavenging kindling wood, and a couple who have just loaded their truck begin to dip into *my* bin. Before I can grab a stick with which to menace them, they start loading the wood into my car. "We got nothing to do for a few minutes." My wife and I sign our mortgage papers and ask for the keys to our new home. "We don't have any," say the sellers. "How do you lock your doors?" "We don't have locks either." This all takes some getting used to, but it's a pleasant acclimation. Less pleasant is the adjustment of a former student, who writes to me today from Pennsylvania and confesses with some embarrassment that he's learned the hard way to lock his car doors. He says he'll be home for Christmas. I had no doubt of that. My question is, Will he leave home again after New Year's Day?

When he heard that I had moved to the Northeast Kingdom, a friend of mine recalled his roommate at Middlebury who had grown up in Orleans village. "Every day he would wake up, and before he said 'Good morning' or put on his pants or anything, he'd cut loose with the longest, meanest string of obscenities and curses I ever heard." I think my friend assumed that his roommate swore because he'd grown up in Orleans. It's more likely that he swore because he had woken up in Middlebury and remembered where he was.

The pull of home, aside from any of home's benefits or college's difficulties, is a pull to be back where "life" is continuing in its customary patterns. Yeats, when he felt the opposite pull, wrote:

> That is no country for old men. The young
> In one another's arms, birds in the trees

—Those dying generations—at their song,
The salmon-falls . . .

It sounds like Orleans village, where the salmon jump the
falls each spring, and "the young in one another's arms" are
soon married, employed, and taking their place behind the
dying generations. The kid who comes home from college for
Christmas to hear of his friends' engagements, or at Easter
to watch the salmon jump, must at times wonder if this is
not his or her true country, instead of the frivolous yet demanding world of college. We have an idea of college as a
kind of saturnalia adorned by books, a place of youthful
indulgence and excess. The idea is partly true; were it not
true, my students would study more easily in their dorms.
But the other side of that truth, perhaps its explanation, is
that college may be one of the last institutions in our culture,
not counting monasteries and convents, where self-denial
is justified in the name of a future reward. It is a little
island of "wait" in a great sea of "now." The wait may
seem unreasonable to a kid who has few educated people
to emulate and many loans to pay off. The "now" of a job
and a family may be powerfully attractive for one who has
grown up in a place where *Our Town*, aside from the sexual innocence of its younger characters, reads like a topical
play.

And so a number come home for good, or transfer to a
school closer to home. I meet them in the store or at the gas
station, and they tell me, "I decided to take a year off." I do
not say, "You'll never go back," any more than I would say
so to a married friend who told me, "We decided to try
separation for a while." There's a Yiddish proverb: "If you
don't sleep under their bed, you don't know their affairs."
And if I don't sleep in their dorms or sit at their desks, how
do I know or how can I judge what sent them home? I tell

them it is never too late to reenroll, and that I will always be happy to help them do so.

Lately I tell my graduating seniors that I wish they would call or write to me before leaving college for good. I owe that advice to one of my students. Several years ago a girl came with the news that her sister was ready to quit college. Her bags were packed. She would have been home already, except that a solicitous roommate had hidden her keys. The younger girl asked if I'd write to her sister. "She always respected you," she said.

Respected or not, I found it hard to believe that she would want to hear from me. Our relationship in composition class had seemed a matter of my writing, "This, too, is a comma splice," and of her thinking, This, too, shall pass. Nevertheless I wrote that same day. My study halls were glad to see me so preoccupied.

The letter was long, and I recall almost none of it. I do remember that I spent at least as much time discussing the academic decisions of my life, both good and bad, as I spent discussing hers. I urged her to stay on, at least for a while longer. I also told her that she should never be ashamed to meet me on the street and look me in the eye and say she had quit. We were talking about the merits of a decision, not the worth of a person. I doubt I said so that succinctly.

She stayed in college. I did not hear from her all semester. I am sure she was struggling to regain the ground she'd lost while packing her bags. And it is no sweet prospect to write to a man who has read your every word to him clutching a red pen.

She came to school on the day before Christmas break, when our students were anticipating the holiday with lovely pagan abandon. She gave me a Christmas card, a letter full of thanks, and a shirt box stuffed with homemade cookies and other treats. I saw her sporadically after that. She was spending more and more of her vacations away from home in order to round out her background with additional courses. She was pretty sure now that she wanted to be a commercial artist.

Then it seemed she was gone for good. But she reappeared at my desk again last year, just before Easter, so changed—and so tan—that I almost didn't recognize her. She was doing postgraduate study in commercial art at a school in Florida—one of the best, she felt, for the kind of work she wanted to do. I asked her what it had been like adjusting to life "down south," not the south that begins at the last St. Johnsbury exit, but the deep South, below Boston.

She said it had been tough at first, not the southernness, but the noise and glitter and crassness of the city where she was living, a favorite spring-break resort for college students which made the wildest dorms look tame by comparison. There was a lot of easy money, a lot of drugs, a lot that struck her as bizarre. "People walk down the street wearing less than I'd wear to the beach." But she was not complaining, or exaggerating, or—though her tan would have concealed it—blushing. She seemed no more interested in being a shocked country girl than in affecting to be a woman of the world. She *was* intensely interested in her work. By the waters of Babylon she had sat down and sketched.

As at our first reunion years earlier, she left me with a gift. Atop some jelly beans was a letter, and atop the letter was a small brown-and-cream-colored shell. It is hard to classify what she wrote, and I will not quote a word of it. She expressed gratitude, but this was not a letter of thanks. She told me how she had found the shell along the coast, but this was not a letter that explains a gift. More than anything else, this was a letter about a life that has realized the significance of its own experience, about a young woman who knows, utterly without vanity, that she is interesting. It occurred to me from the neatness of the copy and from the clarity of the prose that I was reading a final draft. She had written and revised. It also occurred to me that the letter was of a type with the shell: both were the results of long evolution, both were the very best that their creators had to say on a certain subject, and both, just possibly, were intended to delight the beholder.

I am looking out the window of my room at a cold sun, bare trees, and a swirl of falling snow. If you travel some distance in the line of my vision you will see little else until you come to Barton, and beyond that, through more trees and snow, to the school where I teach. I have several letters of recommendation to write before the day is over. One is for Harvard. As I often do when in need of inspiration or courage, I am clutching a seashell in my left hand, sometimes so tightly that I can feel the salt water with my eyes.

A Lover's Quarrel

And were an epitaph to be my story
I'd have a short one ready for my own.
I would have written of me on my stone:
I had a lover's quarrel with the world.

—ROBERT FROST, "The Lesson for Today"

*T*wo years ago, a story appeared in a local newspaper about those who had been named Teacher of the Year for schools in our district. Not far from a photograph that shows me wearing what Emerson calls "the gentlest asinine expression" is the statement "Mr. Keizer loves teaching." I don't think I said that. But since all recipients of such awards seem to say that, the reporter possibly thought I had, or at least saw no harm in saying that I had. And there was no harm inasmuch as I do indeed love teaching, but with a love that makes me hesitate to profess it.

When people, especially other teachers, saw that "quotation," I wonder if they thought what I think when I see similar quotations elsewhere. Who is this person, smiling benignly in front of the blackboard, who *loves* teaching? Is he or she a liar, a simpleton, or a saint? I hope I am neither of the first two, and I know I am not the third. And thus I know that I cannot say I love teaching without a slight, accusing quiver in the pit of my stomach. Robert Frost had a lover's quarrel with the world. I have one with my job.

So do many other people in many other walks of life. Before quarreling publicly, I might do well to remember something Dr. Johnson said: "Every man recounts the inconveniences of his own station, and thinks those of any other less, because he has not felt them." And so I don't say that the inconveniences of another station are less than mine. I only say that mine are considerable. My quarrel is strong.

It is almost as strong as the disaffection of some high school dropouts. I suppose that makes me a sympathetic persuader for staying in school. I had one boy in study hall who would come to my desk and recount all the woes of his station in life. Mrs. C—— was forcing him "to learn all them verbs"— to be followed, no doubt, by all them pronouns—and his father was in league with Mrs. C——. "All I want to do is drop out and go to work in the woods. All I'd need then is a chain saw and a good team of horses." Later his dream changed to being an over-the-road truck driver. When he had finished describing the sweet, schoolless freedom of the road, I would tell him about the sour and probably truckless life of the dropout. Now that he has graduated, would he ever believe that there are mornings when I wistfully imagine him seated on a diner stool, or two (he was huge), sopping up his egg and looking out to where his rig shines red in the dawning sun? "This is for you," he says, handing the waitress an extravagant tip. "What's this for?" she asks suspiciously. "This is because I don't have to write a composition today."

"Yeah, and this is because I don't have to correct it," say I, laying down *my* big tip and rising to join my buddy at the register.

So much has been written—and ignored—about the burden of a high school English teacher's paperwork that I was tempted not to mention it in my quarrel. By now, we've all seen the computations—so many students times so many pages, or so many pages multiplied by so many hours—which prove how much time an English teacher spends correcting, or how little time he or she spends with individual students. I'll only add that nothing in my job brings me closer to quitting. It kills those consolations which make many jobs bearable: a sense of accomplishment, a sense of closure, and a sense of life after work. For in correcting papers I accomplish little for each student, I am never getting done, and I am living only at the cost of neglecting, and thereby accumulating, more papers. I think of Mr. Rochester courting Jane Eyre while his mad wife lurked in the attic. I carve my Thanksgiving turkey or play ball with my daughter—and then there's that chilling laughter upstairs. The papers.

"The worst," says Edgar in *King Lear*, "is not / so long as we can say 'This is the worst.' " The worst part of many troubles, what comes after we have said, "This is the worst," is having people tell us, "This is your own fault." English teachers—all teachers in some way or other—hear a lot of that. We are told that scrupulously reading, commenting, and correcting do no good. We spend too much time. Of course, no one's going to pay out grant money to have some researcher say that we have too many students. No, we spend too much time. We ought to read essays at random, comment sparingly, grade none or one. Probably some of the people making these suggestions know some things I don't. Probably a few more gave up looking for topic sentences long ago and began looking for a rationalization instead. What irritates me are the ones who wouldn't even sharpen a pencil without an airtight publishing contract or the promise of tenure who dare to tell me that teenagers ought to write as though god-inspired because "writing is its own reward." Often kids do just that, but they count on being read at least as diligently as they have written. I don't agree with Dr. Johnson when he says that "no one but a blockhead ever wrote for anything but money." But I do think no one but a blockhead suggests that teachers can get a student to work harder than they are willing to work themselves. In the present system, excellence for one's students comes only at the cost of violence to one's self.

It also irritates me when blockheads belittle an English teacher's preoccupation with correcting matters of form—the nitpicking that "makes kids hate writing" and fills them with pedestrian notions and existential dread and heaven knows what else. These are the same characters who'll sit in the faculty pub and laugh uproariously at the "hick-isms" of any one of my students who fails to master the usage handbook from cover to cover. When I was in graduate school, a noted critic, who needless to say had made his reputation on a dozen or so books all written in standard English, came to tell us how and why standard English was all for the birds. It was a mighty fat and well-plumed bird that said so.

And if our critics can dishearten me, our spokespersons can do worse. It is no easy thing to "regard yourself as a *professional*" while holding a pair of pom-poms and shouting, "Hooray teachers!" It is a hard thing, if not an impossible thing, to "be proud of what you do" while letting go of some of the very attributes that define what you do: a sense of reserve, a capacity for self-criticism, and a standard of service that belongs to you alone. I'm sure what I'm about to say has as much to reveal about my own psychology as it does about the self-defeating character of our self-promoting rhetoric, but the more "praised" and "esteemed" I am, the more ashamed and depressed I feel. We may be on the verge of "a new day for education," but frankly, I cringe at the mention of it.

Perhaps a reason for my cringing, as well as a cause of many a lover's quarrel with my job, is my distaste for "education." Except for the names of medical procedures I might have to undergo, few words make me as queasy as that one. When it does not smack of the most shameless professional jingoism, it bespeaks all kinds of mediocrity, fadism, and quackery; it categorizes all kinds of people who have little to do with what I do in the classroom. For "education" often consists of one desperate swimmer called a teacher and up to a dozen former swimmers or people too proud to swim at all who have managed to clamber onto the teacher's back by becoming administrators, bureaucrats, consultants, "educators" of one sort or another. Every so often my colleagues and I get trained by someone from a state department of education or the education department of a college. I usually sit as far to the back of the room as possible, where I grade papers and wait for "the slip." "The slip" occurs when the trainers says, "Back when I was in a high school classroom . . . "—i.e., before I had the good fortune to get out. I picture them "back in a classroom," wondering, as they are now making *me* wonder, if there isn't some better way to earn a living. I don't despise these people. In fact, I've seen very few that I didn't like. What I despise is that these are the people who get their hands on grants and microphones. These are the people who give counsel in the captain's quarters while the rest of us teeter on the yardarms.

I think the definitive illustration of my resentment is that of a Vermont principal, a former teacher, who decided that her staff was using the office photocopier too often to duplicate tests and exercises. So, she had her secretary type a one-sentence memo to that effect, run off thirty full-page photocopies of the same, and deposit one in each of her teachers' mailboxes. Photocopiers and secretaries are administrative tools. You get to use them by becoming something more important to "education" than a teacher.

In an interview for the Vermont Teacher of the Year competition, I was asked what I found most difficult in my job. I am surprised that I did not answer "grading papers." Perhaps the nature of the competition prompted me to respond: "The struggle not to be cynical." That was not a cynical reply, however. A good part of the struggle not to be cynical is resisting the disheartenment of working in "education." A greater part of the same struggle is resisting the misanthropy which tempts anyone who is compelled by conviction or vocation to love human beings.

A new girl is coming into my study hall. I am forewarned of her. "She's coming from some ugly situations. She's been abused. Her father—mother's boyfriend, whatever—used to hold her bare feet in pans of boiling water. She may have a little trouble relating to men." Oh really? How do I tell her that I will scold her if she creates a disturbance but that I couldn't really blame her if she opened my head with a hatchet? It is all too familiar—what I call "the lowest-dungeon syndrome." In medieval prisons the most hateful criminals were given the lowest dungeon, which served as the cesspool for the other cells. The lowest dungeons in our society are called children. The issues that we read about in *Time,* and discuss over cocktails, and digest after dinner—their waste runs into a kid who in turn runs into a classroom. The legislature passes a tougher child-support law and adjourns. The lawyers pull out the law's teeth and run for the legislature. The sociology professors discuss changing trends in the family and order another salad. But every day the girl with scalded feet gets out of bed and comes to school and sits two yards from my desk, burdened, twisted, hoisted and let fall by a score of halfhearted commitments—from those of the Congress of the United States to those of a man and woman who copulated one night fifteen years ago because there was nothing left to drink.

"Damn teachers. Hate the teachers. Gonna kill the teachers"—the teacher manages to hold the boy in a chair. His anger is not so remarkable as the fact that he hasn't even seen a teacher until a few days ago. He is five years old. He came to school already knowing that he hated it. He can hardly speak a complete sentence. He is furious because the teacher has been trying to show him how to bounce a ball. It's too hard for him. He lives in garbage and dog dung with his brother, mother, and a man who lost his own children for molesting them. "Dad" works at home with his buddy, a fellow pedophile. The heat has gone off in the house. The mother huddles near the kitchen stove with a black eye. A car motor sits in the bathtub. A social worker comes to the door and the mother, who has made some faint overtures for help, is too frightened to open it. The social worker never returns. Only the school bus comes by faithfully, and in a decade, if the boy is still alive, he will come to my school. What disturbs me is not an anguished inner cry of "How can this be?" or a raging inner cry of "This shouldn't be!" but a question that passes over me as calmly as a spring breeze, yet chills me to the bone: "For us to rescue this boy, assuming we thought the rescue possible and the boy worth it, how many pedophiles and millionaires would have to die?"

I am not proud of that thought. I am not proud of many things in my teaching. In the end, one's loathing of anyone else is not so hard to bear as the loathing of one's self. Being a teacher, even more than being a pupil, is a continual coming to judgment. For every weakness, every error, every lapse of a teacher reverberates through twenty captive human beings. I make a humorous remark and realize afterward how precisely it fits—and cuts—a person I never wanted to hurt. I indulge in one digression too many, the point of the day's lesson is lost, and I realize I'm the same little twit who had to raise his hand every two minutes in sixth-grade history class, except that now by sheer endurance I've managed to get the floor and hold on to it. I show my class the filmstrip of *Oedipus Rex* and gape in recognition at the eyeless king who has discovered after ruthless searching what I discover effortlessly day after day, that the source of some pollution, the root of some disorder, the cause of some failure in my classroom is I.

I should love this? Who but a liar, a simpleton, or a saint stands grinning in front of a blackboard and says, "I love teaching"?

If I love teaching, it is with the same desperate, unsentimental, and at times involuntary love that I have for living itself. Like the life of which it forms so large a part, my job absorbs me, nourishes me, and wounds me; it says "I am all there is to existence" at the same time that it urges me to believe in a better one. A single moment of the ecstasy it can provide outweighs a whole year's drudgery; a single accident, a single indiscretion can spoil its sweetness forever. I know I am blessed to partake of it, and I know just as well that I shall have neither rest nor peace until it is done.

And yet, one of the things I find most attractive in teaching is the courage we must show in the face of tasks and conditions that are so dubiously lovable. It is a courage we can sometimes learn from our students. It seems to come more easily to them, perhaps because they are young, and perhaps because the dubiously lovable face of a school has been simplified for them. It is our face, the teacher's face, Mrs. C—— with all them verbs. What I perceive as a bewildering tangle of social injustices and unread essays, of philosophies and follies, is for my students a pair of glasses and a beard, a painted fingernail and a bracelet jangling against the slate. They learn to face us with courage as the personification of all that makes for school. Older and more aware than they, we need to face school and all it comprises, both good and bad, with a courage that justifies their own.

And it is sometimes thrilling to do so. To talk about Aeschylus against all the odds of forgetfulness or indifference, to hold fast to some notion of fairness against the erosion of sly excuses and legitimate exceptions, to resist the impulse to show anger, to maintain that the material will be covered in spite of intercoms, special assemblies, and one's own digressions, to hold a sense of humor in reserve against a sense of futility, to remember what my department head says, that "these kids are not finished products," and then to remember that neither am I—there is a certain gallantry to that. It is a gallantry I miss probably more often than I show, but knowing it exists and is attainable makes my "lover's quarrel" just that: the quarrel of a lover, not the grumblings of a cynic.

This year I am writing a list of meditations to read to myself at the start of each school day. One of them says: "It is not their fault that you teach." Luckily, I do not most days look at my job to see whose fault it is. But there is an insidious trap that catches even the best of us, and once in it we are ready to believe, however vaguely, that a class of twenty freshmen with twenty combs and twenty pieces of bubble gum is entirely responsible for everything from original sin to Monarch Notes. Then we are thinking like that kid who sees the teacher's hand in every schoolish evil from doorless toilet stalls to government-issue beans. We are losing our courage. I think that in other walks of life one's adulthood may often be a thing taken for granted. In teaching it is a thing ever threatened and defended.

I have written as though the code of the teacher as quarreling lover consisted in maintaining a certain stoicism in the face of the unlovable dimensions of our work. But there is also a "soft" courage without which the other kind becomes a vice. This is the courage to surrender.

We need to surrender, first of all, to our own compassion. And we usually do, whether we want to or not. There's a beautiful passage in *King Lear*, where the outraged king has just finished calling on the hurricanes to shatter the world. Having cried out his anger, he turns to behold his fool shivering in the rain.

> Come on, my boy. How dost, my boy? Art cold?
> I am cold myself . . .

Poor fool and knave, I have one part in my heart
That's sorry yet for thee.

And so they take shelter. How often, too, the teacher who
has just raged at "ingrateful man" and the "thick rotundity"
of our educational system turns to behold a wet, shivering
student. My boy, we are both cold in this place called school.
And I have one part in my heart . . .

Once I was called out into the hall where two girls, sisters
as it happened, were fistfighting. I had broken up a few fights
in the past, but this was my first girl-fight, and perhaps for
that reason the most dangerous. Boys spend some time squar-
ing off and exchanging epithets. There's almost something
Homeric about their fighting if one allows that "Ajax, son
of the ancient line of Telamon, when you try me you try no
callow boy or woman innocent of war" has been translated
to "Alex, you goddamn son of a bitch, I'll fucking kill you!"
But the ritual is the same: a little preface that permits either
opponent to run or one of the gods to intervene. When boys
do start to fight, their fists are up in front of their faces. Girls,
on the other hand, have been taught less about bellicose
posturing and self-defense. Their fights are almost entirely
freestyle *offense,* making them a real danger to each other
and, no less significantly, a real danger to an uncoordinated
thirty-year-old with glasses.

With as much caution and delicacy as possible I got the
girls apart and into my empty classroom. Why the tussle?
They were fighting over a tube of lipstick. I told the girls to
look at each other, and I told them that time and chance
were going to do a lot better job of beating the daylights out
of a sister than they ever could, and that in the interim they
just might consider sharing cosmetics. But as I made them
look at each other, they compelled me to look at them. Two
sisters fighting over lipstick—it was the stuff of misanthropic
satire, and yet all I felt was an overwhelming compassion. It

was a lovers' quarrel they were having, and one that illuminated my own. For I, too, have fought my calling and my students, often over nothing more important than a tube of lipstick. I saw one of the girls the other day and she said, "Mr. Keizer, you should put our fight into your book." It was as if she had made the same surrender, and beheld the shivering fool who is sometimes one's sister, and always one's self.

A similar surrender occurred in one of my study halls where I had permitted three boys to play cards—*if* they did not talk. This was against my better judgment, but I had grown tired of watching them yawn and scratch and study pieces of floating lint, and felt that poker might at least be something in the way of mental stimulation. Of course they could not be quiet, though they tried. One period, when I was giving a student extra help in composition, and after I'd been distracted several times by the cardplayers, who winced apologetically and laid fingers to their lips each time I glared, I blew up. No more cards! Cards were through! I was stupid to have allowed cards in the first place. I wasn't going to have studies interrupted by a crummy game of cards. I never wanted to see a card in that study hall again. I didn't even want to hear the *word* "card." "Ace" was no longer an acceptable nickname. All boys named Jack were now to be called John. I wanted them to go through every dictionary in the room and cross out the verb "deal." Was I clear? Did everyone understand my feeling about c-a-r-d-s? Good!

The next day one of the players came to my desk, raised his eyebrows inquiringly, and in the manner of one displaying a dead pheasant, held up a plastic bag full of checkers. You see, I'd said nothing about checkers. There it was—the determination Frost said would take us over the tree fallen in the road, the ice cream sundae that someone invented because other desserts were forbidden on the Sabbath. Poor fool and knave, I have one part in my heart that's sorry—and grateful—yet for thee. I laughed so hard I fear I frightened the kid. Yes, he could play checkers—*if* he didn't talk. Of course I knew he'd talk eventually, but not on that day. And sufficient to that day was the quiet thereof.

Laughter, as well as compassion, calls for a teacher's surrender and keeps the quarrel with one's job loving. We have all heard teachers tell funny stories about their work. What we may not realize is the grace of the laughter when the story happened—the explosion that might have been of another kind were it not for some fortuitous mistake or antic. My heartiest laugh came in a freshman English class that was reading *Macbeth* aloud. Macbeth asks a pair of desperate men if they can bring themselves to murder Banquo and his young son. One of the murderers was played by a boy who was already exhibiting the acting talent that would distinguish him in several school productions. With woeful conviction he read the lines:

> I am one, my liege,
> Whom the vile blows and buffets of the world
> Have so incensed that I am reckless what
> I do to spite the world.

—except that he pronounced "buffet" to rhyme with "soufflé." I was immediately struck by the image of a man driven by one gelatin mold salad too many to commit murder. I laughed like an idiot. I looked at my students and laughed all the more, imagining what *they* were imagining. "Must be one of those dirty parts you have to be a friggin' English teacher to understand." "You know, this is what happens to you when you read too much of that stuff." It is indeed what comes of reading "that stuff," and of rereading it in the company of young men and women: laughter, rich, abundant laughter that enables a sullen English teacher to picture himself rising in ludicrous wrath at some education luncheon to say that he is through with vile blows and buffets.

The last kind of "soft" courage, the last and probably the most difficult of a teacher's vital surrenders, is to accept success where it is not deserved, and when all of the deserved successes have failed to come about.

One day my department head told me, "Something you said in Bible as Literature sure made an impression on Kristine. She came in here to talk to me, and boy, it sure gave her something to think about."

I couldn't wait to hear what I had said to make so great an impression. We were in the middle of final exams, and I was learning by the hour that some of what I say makes no impression whatsoever. One student evaluation read: "Your a good teacher Mr. Keizer," which only wanted the word "English" in between "good" and "teacher" to make the irony complete. But what had touched this student? Was it some quotation from the theophany in Job, from the Torah, from the Sermon on the Mount? Was it the implications of ethical monotheism for Western civilization, the assertion of matter's goodness in the face of the Gnostic challenge, the passion of the rhapsodic prophets for social justice, the passion of Solomon for his beloved, the humor of the Hasidic masters, the tragedy of Saul, the horror of the Holocaust, the sublimity of Vedanta or Zen?

"You told an anecdote"—ah, which one?—"about a man"— ah, which man?—"a friend of yours, and you identified him as 'probably my best friend, after my wife.' She couldn't get over your calling your wife your best friend."

This Kristine was a teenaged wife and mother; apparently her husband's opinion was that he'd done her his best and last favors by making her both. That her marriage to him entitled her to the prerogatives of his friendship was a radical idea to Kristine—perhaps more so than any other of the ideas that have shaped our consciousness as heirs to the Judeo-Christian tradition. I suppose I should have thrown my lecture notes out the window and started a degree in marriage counseling. But on that day I had the sense to be no more than abashed and grateful.

E. B. White wrote: "No one should come to New York unless he is willing to be lucky." No one should come to teaching unless he is willing to be unlucky, and lucky, and surprised so often and so profoundly that any notion of luck or its lack—of love or of hate for one's work—rests on the shakiest ground.

The Question of Merit Pay
and the Legend
of Harriet the Cook

> "He makes his cook his merit . . . "
> —MOLIÈRE, *The Misanthrope*

A much debated issue in education at this time is that of merit pay. Most teachers oppose the idea, and I imagine that many outsiders interpret that stance as a tacit admission of meritlessness. These teachers, they feel, are afraid they'll have to start working for their money.

I, too, oppose merit pay. Yet, I am bold enough to think that I'd get a healthy raise if it became policy. I hope one valid reason for my thinking so is that I am a good teacher. Were that the only reason, I might think merit pay a good idea. But other reasons, entirely irrelevant to my teaching abilities, would serve to make me "meritorious."

For one thing, I'm seasoned enough to have proven my value, but young enough not to be taken for granted. My seven years' experience would not price me above the means of another school district if I should wish to change jobs. I have no relatives in the area, no children in school, no health problems. Were I forty-seven, born and raised in the area, with twenty years of teaching experience, two kids in the schools, another at college, a mother in a local nursing home, a bad case of smoker's cough, and all the pedagogical merits of Socrates himself, I might not have the prospects I do now.

Remember, we speak of merit pay as an "incentive," and incentives rarely go to those without choices.

I also teach high school, which means that I'm well placed to take credit for achievements that are the result of cumulative teaching efforts. Last year my freshman student Jessica Davis took a first prize of a thousand dollars in the Vermont Honors Competition for Excellence in Writing. I taught composition in Jessica's English class, and when we learned of her candidacy, I gave her extra coaching outside of class, which she graciously acknowledged in the newspaper articles about her. But the fact is, I did not make Jessica Davis a good writer. Somewhere on the scale of merit between me and God are at least eight elementary school teachers. The University of Vermont, which sponsors the competition, did make general acknowledgment of their efforts in its communication with our school. And my department head took it upon herself to send them letters of congratulation. But who was invited to feast in the faculty dining room at the University with Jessica and her parents, and ate more than all three combined? I was a little full then, but after listening to a few speeches and taking a few sips of mineral water, I could have made room for a generous slice of merit pay.

Finally, most of my students are in the upper levels. That means they generally do well, and the "merit" of what I teach them is more likely to show up in things like standardized tests, competitions, college report cards, and decent jobs. It also means that their parents are usually concerned about education, likely to appear at school functions, talk to school administrators, perhaps serve a term on the school board. In a merit pay plan executed within the present school-society framework, every teacher would need to toot his or her own horn—but some of us could count on a full brass band besides.

I wonder how I'd do in competition with some of my colleagues, with those in special education, for instance. In a school not far from mine, a teacher ran a class for learning-impaired students. One of them periodically came to school in such filth that the teacher was distracted from her duties, which is a euphemistic way of saying that she often ran the risk of adding the smell of fresh vomit to the stench of dried feces. So before the school day began, she changed into a bathing suit, took the boy into a shower, bathed him, and changed his clothes. I don't know if that qualifies as merit or not, but I'd be interested in knowing who would say so if it did. The child's mother, who lacked the means, the concern, or possibly the IQ to use a bar of soap? The school principal, who might have been just as happy to see the whole retarded outfit gone so he could use the classroom for something important, like the storage of athletic equipment? The kid, if by chance he learned to talk? Who would? Or is the real question, Who cares?

There are other cases of merit I can cite that will be news to many in our own community no less than to a distant reader. Almost every morning of every summer a friend of mine, also a special education teacher, tutors students in their homes. He does not ask for compensation. I am not even sure that the school administration knows what he's doing. Friends urge him to ask for mileage money at the very least. He claims the red tape would be too much of a bother. And I've never known him to answer anything other than "Yes it is" when someone accosts him with "Gee, it must be nice to have the whole summer off."

Another teacher, who works in a local elementary school, starts her summer by tearing up every note, exercise, and handout that she has used to teach the preceding year. In the fall, she will begin from scratch. Just the thought that I might be forced by theft or fire to adopt this woman's standards makes me light-headed. How does one quantify that kind of integrity?

As I write, one of our first-grade teachers is adjusting the last hem of the authentic Pilgrim costumes she has sewn for *every* student in her class. A girl so poor that she has on occasion come to school without underwear stands smoothing down the folds of her long dress in wonderment. "See my dress!" she calls out to the visitor. It may be the cleanest, newest, handsomest thing she has ever worn—this garment of another age's austerity. How many hours this teacher must have spent at home behind a sewing machine—how many seconds will it take to punch her dedication into someone's business-model, performance-oriented, incentive-based, computerized version of how schools ought to run?

Admittedly, all of the examples one can use to point out the shoddiness of an idea like merit pay can also be used to question the present salary system, which essentially rewards people year after year for remaining certifiable as teachers and living tissue. Granted that some of the people I cite could miss out on merit pay. What extra reward are they getting now?

To broach that question and to conclude my discussion, it might be well advised to step aside somewhat from my own job—not out of school, just out of the teachers' lounge. And so by way of analogy, I close with the Legend of Harriet the Cook.

For a number of years, Harriet was cook at an elementary school in the Northeast Kingdom. Its playground is bordered by a fence, on the other side of which are grazing cows, and beyond them, a valley and a range of beautiful wooded hills. I like to think that Harriet could see all of this from the cafeteria windows and that she enjoyed the view. She didn't make much money. If she was sick, it was her responsibility to find—and pay—her own substitute. Her town is not well known for school expenditures, for *any* kind of expenditures. I haven't changed Harriet's name, but I'm not worried about the world's beating a path to her door for the simple reason that most of the world lacks the strength of stomach or automotive suspension to take all the potholes on the way.

I first learned about Harriet through my wife, whose job as speech pathologist often took her to Harriet's school. She always considered herself fortunate when her appointments fell around lunch. One afternoon she encountered an irate and breathless little boy running upstairs from the locked school kitchen with fists clenched.

"I'm gonna kill that Billy," he gasped.

"Whoa. What's wrong?" my wife said.

"Well, he"—*breathe, breathe, breathe*—"was supposed to give Harriet my lunch money for tomorrow"—*swallow, breathe, breathe*—"and he forgot to do it, and Harriet just went home for the day"—*choke, sob*—"and I'm just gonna kill him!"

The reader who calls this nothing but childish hysteria should know that we're talking about fresh corn muffins, breast of turkey straight from the bird, pan gravy, garden vegetables, and a choice of two desserts. In short, we're talking about what was probably the best and very likely the first meal of that child's day. In a similar position, I might have killed Billy, too, except for my trusting Harriet to cook a little extra just in case.

Harriet's reputation as a home-style school cook reached me through other sources. I taught high school seniors who remembered her cooking fondly, though they had last tasted it in fourth grade. Most of what Harriet had to work with was the same government-issue stocks that come to other schools, but apparently she exercised some alchemical power over them. I do know that she often used vegetables from her own home garden. I have not been able to discover how her turkey came off a bird, while turkey at many schools and some restaurants comes off something called a "loaf," which if I were a turkey I'd sue for defamation of character. At snack time, Harriet set out individual trays, each marked with a student's name; on special occasions students received personalized gingerbread men. Once the school was without electricity for three days. Whether Harriet liked a challenge or simply disliked cold sandwiches, I don't know, but during the blackout she took home cooking to extremes—by taking it home, all of it, and driving it back to school hot and on time for lunch.

It was not simply Harriet's cooking that was so uncompromisingly home-style, but the whole atmosphere of her kitchen. I have heard from those who visited the school that it was not uncommon to find a student seated on a countertop amid mixing bowls and aluminum foil and reading aloud while Harriet corrected mispronunciations as deftly as she peeled potatoes. She was cook, tutor, and a living rewards system as well. A colleague recalls an underachiever succeeding at last in the form of a good test grade; when class was over, the boy rushed out clutching his paper—and made straight for the kitchen door.

People like Harriet present special difficulties when we begin to talk about things like jobs and pay. If there were such a thing as a school cooks' union, say a National Nutrition Association, I'm sure that some of its members would view Harriet as a not-too-distant relation to the scab family— "She makes the rest of us look bad"—though doubtless the same individuals would be quick to cite "people like Harriet" with demands for a higher wage. And if the government published a study on the crisis in school lunch programs, *Stomachs at Risk,* and if politicians suddenly discovered that hot lunch could be hot politics, they too would cite Harriet as the *raison d'être* for a scheme like merit pay—that is, if someone were kind enough to inform them of Harriet's existence. As a possibility they might grasp her; as a person they would never come near her.

As both of our hypothetical factions tossed the hapless

cook back and forth, they would reveal by degrees their un-willingness to face the mystery of a Harriet. For the truth is, Harriet will exist or not exist irrespective of anybody's money. None of us wants to admit that, for if true, it means that the universe, or at least that part of the universe in which Harriet baked her muffins, is somewhat beyond our understanding; worse yet, beyond our control; and worst of all, beyond our opportunism. It is likely that we do lose a Harriet now and then by failing to pay her what she needs to survive. It is less likely that we attract a Harriet by money. It is unlikely to impossible that we create one that way.

That last disconcerting truth was put bluntly to me by a school principal with whom I interviewed for a job. He in-troduced his school's salary schedule this way: "Now as far as money goes, if you're a teacher you don't care about money. You teach because you care about kids." This is the same man who asked me out of the blue if I was a Communist and *happily* married—the latter because he didn't want me "running around feeling the girls"—and I've always regretted that I didn't put my hand gently on his thigh and say, "Not to worry, Comrade Principal . . . " My point is that even a person of his low caliber knew about the priceless dedication that makes a good teacher or, for that matter, a good school cook. Managers and administrators of his caliber *always* know about such dedication. It is their stock-in-trade to take ad-vantage of it. And it would be their role to define and reward merit—and to do so within a system that judged *their* merit by how well they managed to attract "good people" whose primary motivation is never money to begin with.

This brings us to a place where we might evaluate the idea of merit pay realistically. As an idea it makes some sense. For teachers to claim that there are no reliable criteria for setting salaries other than years of experience and education is something akin to claiming that justice is too complex for mortal administration, and so sentencing should be done entirely by "schedule" without the services of a judge. Put more simply, it is to ally ourselves with the principal mentioned above and say that since Harriet works irrespective of salary, our salary schedules ought to be written irrespective of Harriet. We ought to assume that her excellence is a fluke, or maintain that it comes from experience, or pretend that we're all just as excellent as she. In our heart of hearts we know that's wrong. We know the present system contains as many injustices as it prevents.

But we also know that even if some of the thinking behind merit pay is sound, the spirit behind it is frequently cynical and cheap. We sense—quite accurately, I think—that the merit-pay proponent does not want to compensate a Harriet so much as humiliate, divide, and conquer "all the other goof-offs." The proponents of merit pay need to admit that the biggest goof-offs are they. For it is goofing off to be ignorant of a Harriet until it becomes politically expedient to know about one. It is goofing off to think that there are only one or two Harriets and myriads of losers teaching in our schools. It is goofing off to think that merit pay could work without a complete rethinking of school administration and a momentous realignment of schools and their communities.

And, finally, it is goofing off to think that our only obligation to a Harriet is to find out her price. As I said, she has none. That does not mean there is no price to pay, however. When the merit-pay people come to Harriet's kitchen not with a smug little scheme to entice her but with the justice to reward her, not with salary only, but like repentant Scrooges with turkeys as big as the boy on the street—and a microwave oven for the cafeteria, and a set of sharp knives—then perhaps they will have begun to back their rhetoric with money and their money with moral force. Until teachers see a true change of heart among the politicians, educational consultants, and general skinflints buzzing around the "excellence" movement, we will never break ranks on the issue of payment.

Even a somewhat renegade teacher like myself will quote the party line until he hears something qualitatively different from a party line. As for a Harriet, she is probably too busy cooking to quote anyone's line.

Not everyone is a Harriet, of course. When all school cooks are Harriet, all physicians are Dr. Schweitzer, all funeral directors are Joseph of Arimathea, then all teachers will be like the celibate drudge who graces the one-room schoolhouse of our nostalgic dreams. I'm not sure how wonderful such a transformation would be even if it were possible. We need some ordinary human beings with reasonable commitments. We need a few psychiatrists who refuse to take calls at home, if only so that a few of their children might grow up not needing psychiatrists. And we need teachers who treat themselves with as much mercy as criticism, if only so that they can treat their students likewise.

Nevertheless, Harriet is the ideal. There must always be a few of her if the rest of us are to find our way. A few ascetics need to spend their lives raving in the desert in order for the rank and file to make it into church on Sunday. If teachers and public cannot acknowledge both the acceptable rarity and the absolute necessity of Harriets, we are lost.

Someday I will go to see Harriet the Cook, whom I have never met. I shall need to go to her home. Two years ago she retired. A few students, teachers, and parents took a collection, commissioned an artist, and presented Harriet with an oil painting of her school which shows the children playing in the yard, and the mountains Harriet may have been able to see from the cafeteria. It will be a while before I go. I am not ready yet for the desert; I am not even ready for the potholes. I'm not sure how I will arrange our meeting or what I will say to her. I have worked out only a few details. I will call beforehand. I will wear a tie. I will take a gift. And I think I will go in November, sometime between All Saints' Day and Thanksgiving, and as close to lunch as possible.

The Gospel of Unfairness

" 'But when this son of yours came, who has devoured your living with harlots, you killed for him the fatted calf!' And he said to him, 'Son, you are always with me, and all that I have is yours. It was fitting to make merry and be glad, for your brother was dead, and is alive; he was lost, and is found.' "

—LUKE

One of the most exciting moments in all of my literature classes, both those I've taken and those I've taught, is the trial of Orestes. The avenging Furies have pursued him to Athens for murdering his mother. Apollo, proud and somewhat arbitrary, has vowed to defend him. Between Apollo's whims and the Furies' inflexibility, between Orestes and his fate, stands Athena, in whose hands the final decision rests.

The play interests my students because it treats a theme which they as students, siblings, and growing children care very much about: fairness. Their lives are often "on trial," or in competition with other lives; so the question of "what is fair" is an important one.

The parable of the prodigal son, the conclusion of which I quote above, also deals with fairness. We read it in my Bible as Literature class, and students show the same interest for much the same reason. Of course, the concerns of Aeschylus and Jesus differ. Aeschylus is concerned with the nature of divine justice; and Jesus, with the nature of divine love. But their conclusions are remarkably similar. Both see the ultimate good, be it conceived as justice or love, as lying beyond simplistic notions of what's fair. It is not fair to acquit Orestes for matricide; it is not fair to treat prodigality with a fatted calf. The Furies in the first story and the elder son in the second are insistent on this point. Nevertheless, Athena and the prodigal son's father see some value beyond the tit-for-tat laws of their respective universes. Whatever it is they're seeing, my students often have a hard time making it out. They want a decision that's *fair*.

In the running of my classroom, so do I. The theme common to the play and the parable is not lost on me, and shortly I shall discuss some of what I think it means; but the truth is, I have taught for seven years with "fairness" as one of my highest priorities. I want to be fair for the simple reason that when students are convinced enough of a teacher's impartiality and sound judgment, they learn better. They make better scholars when they no longer feel the need to double as lawyers. When they become convinced that there are neither pampered favorites to be exposed nor advantageous loopholes to be discovered, they relax and they learn.

Creating that kind of atmosphere is difficult and tentative. If Alice's writing always gets an A and Phoebe hardly ever earns a B, should Phoebe get extra points for a good effort? It seems as though she should—and yet, it may be that Alice is actually an overachiever whose every A has come at a cost to her intestinal lining, whereas Phoebe learned long ago that coming from far behind in the last lap always gets you more cheers than falling back to second place after a three-lap lead.

Moreover, is it fair to make exceptions for "special cases"— problems at home, "personal" difficulties? I sometimes do. I like to believe I'm saying to my student, "I care about your problems and about your life outside of school," but perhaps I'm really saying, "Spill your guts to me and I'll be lenient.

Tell me your story and I'll accept your excuse." How often in schools do we punish—in addition to cheating, insolence, and assault—modesty, independence, and self-respect? And how often have I treated an irresponsible kid better than a responsible one, not because, like the prodigal son's father, I rejoiced to welcome him home, but because I feared my bias would make me unfair? Fairness is no different from any other balancing act; eventually the gyrations we employ to keep us up only bring us down.

And some of the crashes are especially inglorious. Not long ago, two teachers in an area school came before their board with a grant proposal to receive monies set aside by the state or federal government—I forget which—for "gifted and talented" students. Obtaining the grant would have cost the school nothing but the postage on the application; rejecting it would have guaranteed nothing but that another school, probably one less needy, would take the grant instead. Yet, reject the grant the school board did.

Various reasons were given, but the consensus was pretty well summarized by a man who said, in effect, the smart kids will be getting something special, the slow kids are already getting special ed.—what about the kids in the middle? It isn't fair.

There was some bitterness among that school's teachers; I also felt bitter when I heard of the decision. Yet the board had acted in this case as I often act in my classroom, with the almost fanatical aim of being fair. Far from allowing the end to justify the means, I allow the means to obscure the end. Obsessed with fairness—perhaps more from pride than from integrity—I can forget the very reason that compelled me to be fair in the first place. I can forget the learning. One might begin to ask, following the lead of Aeschylus and Jesus, if fairness is always the high ideal we take it for.

Fairness often seems to be—not justice, but the justification of the status quo. A farm mortgage is foreclosed, a river is poisoned, a nine-year-old girl is raped, and we work diligently to see that all parties receive a *fair* hearing. So we should. But we act as though our fairness has earned us the luxury of ignoring the causes and the effects of whatever outrage has taken place. We can excuse ourselves from larger questions of justice by preoccupying ourselves with the minutest matters of form. We can excuse ourselves from asking, "Exactly what kind of a society are we seeking to create?" I suppose the stock reply would be "A fair one." Hardworking people are reduced to penury, rivers are turned to running filth, a child is terrorized, degraded, and scarred—but let it never be said we're not fair. We play by all the rules. We close the case properly. We go home to bed. And is it not in the same spirit of fairness that I close my gradebook on the marking period? I have been scrupulously fair. Do not trouble me with larger questions like "Did anybody learn anything?"

As often as not, we defend being lazy or stingy by claiming to be fair. Fairness is the seal on our limited commitments. What mother or father who loves a child is only fair to that child? What man or woman is fair to a dear friend? We're fair to the coolie who stacks the wood. We're fair to the maid, to the poor—to the school system. What is more, we're fair *through* the school system; we let it be the standard-bearer and the burden-bearer for our halfhearted reforms. We integrated the schools first, as was fitting. But decades later we are still letting our discussions of racial justice center on where black and white kids get off the school bus rather than on what kinds of houses, suppers, and opportunities they get off to. We strike down affirmative-action programs—in the name of fairness! If we're fair in school, we seemingly need not be just, courageous, or visionary anywhere else.

So, when my students come away from the *Oresteia* or the parables saying, "It doesn't seem fair," I'm inclined to answer, "No, it doesn't seem fair to me either. And perhaps we ought to think about that."

Occasionally I do a project in class which allows me to work somewhat beyond fairness. Several times that project has been the making of a book, once it was a play, and for the past two years it has been the production of a single-issue newspaper. These sound like what are usually extracurricular activities, but they interest me for their potential to alter the way a classroom works. Their inclusion within the curricular framework of grading, daily scheduling, and discipline necessitates a rethinking of that framework—something along the lines of "Where does a five-hundred-pound gorilla sleep?" Anywhere it wants. If the students elect to give the ape sleeping room, teacher and student alike will need to work with greater cooperation, flexibility, and abandon than ever before. I shall need to ask things of students and they will need to demand things of me which are not, in the usual way of thinking, "fair."

For that reason, a project like a class newspaper meets with immediate resistance from a few members of the class. Generally, the skeptical are neither the brighter students, who see in the project a chance to run in other than slow motion, nor the low achievers, who see a chance to compensate for what they cannot do by what they are willing to do. And the average students, on the whole, have few complaints. Nevertheless, the typical objectors are people who've been hiding out in the fat part of the bell curve and placing big bets on the opportunity provided by a fair class to earn a fair grade with a fair degree of effort. (If ever I were to praise my native tongue, I'd cite its having the same word to mean one-dimensional justice and mediocrity.) The objectors want to know all possible risks, and they want to take out the full coverage against every one of them. I suppose they would feel more comfortable with our project if I gave them each a contract, spelling out the work and the reward. But I won't raise them above a litigious or timid approach to learning by

making myself into their lawyer or claims agent, or by re-
making them in the image of my unionized teacher self. We're
turning this class into a newsroom, not the town clerk's office.

So I give their questions the fairest answers I can, knowing
full well that we have already begun to leave the domain
where such answers make sense. They want the odds; I'm
giving them possibilities. Their goal is a passing grade; my
goal and the goal of their peers is a surpassing piece of work.
They continue to look for the worst-case scenario until their
peers lose patience or they lose heart. What if we can't find
any news? What if the editors get bossy? What if we don't
finish on time? Can some of us just do "regular" work instead?

My answer to the last is both peremptory and perverse.
"No, you can't. That wouldn't be fair."

As the project gets under way, one notices a variety of
positive changes. Writing gets better. The student is not thinking, What's fair for the teacher to expect? but What's likely
to be demanded by my readers, who will not necessarily be
fair? Peer editing becomes less artificial, less evenly reciprocal—and much more intense. The teacher, who sees the entire
task and its time limits from a better perspective, is now the
likeliest one to say, "This'll have to do." It is the *student* who
agitates for perfection, and who demands it of self and peers.
Most fascinating to observe is the appreciation won by certain
personalities. A shy isolato becomes a leader for the habit of
mind that settles an argument over two different typefaces
by asking if either of the disputants knows how to type. One
still hears her voice only by straining, but one makes it a
point to strain.

Sooner or later it becomes apparent that the paper will
never get out unless we put in some time after school. Of
course I cannot coerce anyone to do so; it is somewhat unfair
of me even to ask. All I can offer are rides, supper, and my
own promise to be there. A number come; a few are prepared

to stay the night if necessary. And what a night it promises to be. Anyone who knows a school by day will understand the peculiar ambience it takes on in the dark, when the last of the athletes has gone home and the light in a classroom is the only one on in the wing. The students and I move giddily within a paradox whereby we have somehow played truant by giving ourselves a detention. We treat one another in a democratic spirit which in the daylight would only seem impertinence on their part and affectation on mine. They use my key for the faculty bathrooms, my desk for their coffee breaks. The room fills with paper cuttings and crumpled pages, all infected with paste. I'm not sure where my gradebook is. A giant nocturnal moth with the markings of an owl shoots through an open window and attacks the fluorescent lights. The clock clicks and we look up to see a new configuration on its face, not the one for lunch or social studies or the bus ride home. It's going on bedtime, and we haven't sent for the pizzas yet.

Still later, high on soda and bylines, we begin to be different people. We begin to assume the same frenetic movements, the same glib camaraderie and wise-guy lingo of those caricaturized newsrooms in black-and-white movies. This is the *Trib* with the latest poop on Mussolini and the paperhanger. This is the seamy world of the Albany gaming rackets, circa 1936. Not Albany, Vermont, mind you. The other Albany. The big one. Billy Keizer's Greatest Game. Where's your green eyeshade, Keizer?

"Come again?"

"I said where the hell's Martin, Mr. Keizer? How come he didn't show?"

"He's on a job. It's his night to bag at the C & C. But Martin's on the level. He says he'll type his own copy if we leave him a hole."

"Yeah, but who's gonna proofread it? I don't wanna sound fussy, but the guy spells like a chimp."

"Take it easy. We got Beverly on that one. She's meeting him after work to read it through."

"Probably not all she's meeting him for."

"Hey, Moe, mind your beeswax. What about your piece? What's its condition?"

"Critical."

"Run it by Linda. If she gives it the high sign, you don't need nothing from me."

The spell is broken—or perhaps enhanced—by a usually personable janitor who barges into the room and all but screams at me that if we're going to be here past eleven, which is his quitting time, we damn well better make sure that outside gate is padlocked, because if it's not, he's going to make sure I take the rap for it. Tough guy. It has been a while since anyone at school has talked to me like that, probably because it's been a while since I've been at school past eleven. The scolding serves as yet another lesson of the whole experience, a review, really, of a principle I learned by observing my teachers long before I became a teacher myself: If you want to get in trouble in a school, take your job seriously. Attempt to break through what is "fair" in every sense of the word. I have a hunch that if we were to make a list of all the public school teachers in any given year who've been reprimanded, fired, or pressured into quitting, we'd find that more of them were in trouble for high standards than for low, more for defending students than for striking them, for challenging students than for seducing them, for exposing folly than for exposing themselves. No, I am not saying that the majority of teachers are conscientious. I am saying that the majority of those who get into trouble probably are. I am saying that the pursuit of this educational excellence that everybody is ballyhooing all of a sudden can be the greatest single liability a teacher assumes. The teacher who takes it easy, who does little enough in class to permit a comfortable roster of duties outside class, who makes a good appearance, who gives a lot of B's—i.e., who's very fair—is much preferable to the frazzled zealot who mistakenly thinks that something is actually going on.

At our school we are luckier than most. Our principal, Mr. Wood, supports this night's marathon and any other eccentricity he deems beneficial for students or teachers. He will be one of the first to buy a newspaper on Monday. But he will read no further than the second column of page one before somebody takes him to task because the photocopier was overused, too many junior reporters were in the office, the paste is all gone, the gate was unlocked for most of the night. The good shepherd lays down his life for the sheep, which, needless to say, isn't fair.

By 1 A.M. most of the students have left. I have been urging them to go for several hours, but they truly want the paper out on time, and all defections past ten have been prompted by orders from home. One mother drove right under the classroom windows and called up cops-and-robbers style for her daughter to come out *now!* Another mother, who's been helping on layout and who left to print more headlines over at the Barton *Chronicle* office, returns with a traffic ticket. "The cop pulled me over because a headlight was out. Across the street there's this whole mob of rowdy guys revving their motors . . . " Her son finishes for her, "And the cops have to go pick on a little old lady." It would appear that there is no longer any fairness left in the world. We laugh.

An hour and a half later, two people remain to inspect the finished mock-ups, not counting the little old lady and me. One has the highest class average; the other, the lowest. One has nothing to gain; the other, nothing to lose. They have worked side by side for two nights that are the equivalent length of four weeks of English classes. As they stand together like gods in jeans on the sixth day of some creation, seeing "it is good" and looking good for it, I see in their juxtaposition "the way things ought to be" but so seldom are. I see how many problems could have been prevented, how many inequalities could have been deemphasized, how many irritations could have become pearls had we done something like this more often, or at least earlier in the year. But I also see a briefcase full of work that has accumulated over weeks of thinking almost nothing but newspaper, I see an upcoming week of exams for which I am ill-prepared, I see a picture in my mind of kids in other classes who have probably been shortchanged by this particular enthusiasm, and I see a picture in my wallet of people I do not see enough. At best, we have merely done a tableau of educational paradise; we have not entered it. Nor will I enter, if this is the cost.

With that thought I realize, or rather I remember, that as often as fairness grows out of laziness or stinginess it also grows out of necessity. It grows out of the recognition that we dispense love or justice as neither Athena nor God. A father or mother who loves a child may indeed be "only fair" to that child, if the child is one of eight, and there is but fifty dollars to spend on Christmas presents. A teacher who loves a student may indeed be only fair to that student, if the student is one of a hundred, and there are but twenty-four hours in a day. And a school board member who truly cares about the kids over whose learning he has been voted a custodian may indeed have to be maddeningly fair about what any group of them gets—even by way of federal grant—when all are getting so little.

It is not fairness I despise, then, so much as our willing acquiescence to necessity—or worse, our creation of artificial necessities to justify our being "only fair." Those who want better schools talk about giving teachers more money; I need it, I deserve it, I'll take it. But what I really need to do the job is time and space and fewer students. What I really want is the liberty to teach abundantly, to be more than just fair to my students while remaining at least fair to myself and to those who share my life.

Finally, I see my gradebook under the clutter, and with it the need to quantify what we have done. I still cannot find where I left my fair standards, though. Earlier that evening I was asked how I intended to grade "all of it." I wasn't sure, I said. It would probably go something like this: You'll receive grades for your articles; the whole class, committed and non-committed, will receive a grade for the newspaper, which would appear to be an A. Those of you who worked "above and beyond" will receive yet another A, though I'm not going to bother distinguishing between eight hours' service and twelve. Is that fair?

They nodded their heads emphatically, especially the kid who had flunked three marking periods in a row. It was fair.

You think so, huh? I said to myself. Well, let me tell you something. Maybe it ain't fair at all. Maybe there's no such thing as fair, see? And maybe I don't give a damn if there is, 'cause for just this once, fair's making itself scarce for a little bit. Fair's got business out of state. Fair's gone to visit its old lady in Schenectady, or Purgatory, I forget which. And you wanna know why? 'Cause we're finishing off the fatted calf tonight, that's why. 'Cause this your brother was a first-class loser, and now he's just first-class. He was a regular stiff, and now he's so spanking alive that just looking at his grinning mug—that's right, I said an A—is enough to give me the heebie-jeebies.

The Parson in Circuit

The Countrey Parson . . . takes occasion sometimes to visit in person, now one quarter of his Parish, now another. For there he shall find his flock most naturally as they are, wallowing in the midst of their affairs.

—GEORGE HERBERT, *A Priest to the Temple*

*F*our years after I began teaching, I was formally installed as the Lay Vicar of Christ Episcopal Church in Island Pond. Several conversions both in myself and in my church enabled that to happen; some are ongoing, none is pertinent to the discussion here. What is very pertinent, however, is that this new work led to a kind of conversion in my teaching. I began to think of my students as a parish and of myself as its parson. I don't think this is an unusual attitude; many teachers probably share it in some form or another, though they may not use the ecclesiastical metaphor. A metaphor is all it is, of course. I am not in school to proselytize, but to encourage learning. My "parish" there is a cure of minds, not a cure of souls. But I am no less a curate for all that.

We tend to speak of our vocations in similes and metaphors—even the parson speaks of himself as an angler, harvester, or shepherd—and the figures of speech we choose reflect and in some cases determine the way we do our work. If my walk through the corridors of a school is hall "patrol," then I am a cop, the school is my beat, and my manner, however polite, is that of a man who packs a gun. But if instead I "make the rounds of the parish," both I and those I meet must adopt a different kind of demeanor. A parson does not say, "And just where do you think you're going, buster?" His parishioner does not reply, "None of your god-damned business." At times each may feel like speaking in just this way, but custom dictates otherwise.

I know this sounds very idealistic—it *is* very idealistic—and I would be the first to admit its limitations. There have been days when one could have come into my school and seen me yanking two furious boys apart in a scene that belonged more to *Fort Apache, the Bronx* than to *The Bells of St. Mary's*. But that I have been able to walk those same boys to the office with my hands on their shoulders instead of around their necks is some proof of the ideal's potential for realization. I might add that I can name men and women in my district who fulfill the ideal much better than I do. My colleague Charlie Powell has converted some of the unlikeliest students to dramatics—tobacco-spitting bruisers to doing en-trechats *in public*—largely by the way he "pastors" his performers day and night. I am not saying that I cut a pastoral figure at my school. I am saying that the standard against which I measure myself, and the imagery with which I try to think of myself, are both pastoral—and that this makes a difference.

Too often the metaphors of education belong to the world of business, if not the world of war. The principal is an "administrator," an "executive," a "chairman of the board," a "captain." I would just as soon think of mine as a bishop, and I would dare to say that my choice of metaphor comes closer to the right vision for a school than these others. The principal is the one who defends the faith of a school, who preserves its best intentions, who blesses its missions, who inspires by the dignity of his office and the charisma of his person more than he threatens by the severity of his commands. He is not a boss set over teachers, but the chief teacher himself, the one who can be trusted above all others to lay down his life for the sheep.

Perhaps this is quaint. Perhaps I teach in a quaint place, but my picture of a school administrator is closer to the spirit of the man and woman under whom I work than is the remark of a principal who once defined teaching for me as "busting heads."

When I speak of teaching as a pastoral activity, I mean first of all that the teacher is of the same "kind" as his students. Just as the parson is not an angel come down from heaven to direct his parishioners, but is a fellow servant with them, so a teacher does not "produce" scholars; he sets an example of scholarship. He learns with his students; he is a student. When I write a letter of recommendation for a young man or woman in the school, I do not say, "I have taught so and so," but "I have studied with so and so," in the same way as a parson might speak of her parishioner not as someone to whom she has preached but as someone with whom she has prayed.

As a parson must pray, a teacher must pursue his interests, nurture his intellectual passions—I am talking about rejuvenation, which is something more and very often something other than recertification. A teacher who so "dedicates" himself to teaching that he abandons the pursuit of the subject he first yearned to teach is one of the most tragic types among us. His opposite, a type too paltry to be tragic, is the one who says, "Well, I'm *really* a poet, but I teach English for a job." How sad to be but part real. I am really an English teacher, and I am really a writer, and I like to think I am more really the one for being the other. I know from experience what it is like for my students to struggle with an essay; I can hear the confessions because I have committed the sins.

To think of oneself as a parson also means that one pursues teaching with a certain disregard for the trivia attached to it. One's eyes are fixed on heaven. Otherwise, it is possible to begin believing that one has actually been hired to form committees and chaperon dances, to parrot rules and write licenses for urination. In other words, it is quite possible for a teacher to put in a hard day's work without having taught much of anything.

I once read of an Orthodox monk whose job it was to supervise a workshop of lay laborers. Instead of walking the floor to check on their work, he retired to an adjoining room and prayed in detail for each of them throughout the shift. Supposedly, his production figures were phenomenal. I'm quite aware of the pious overlay the story has probably received. But I wish that "educators" were just as aware of the very basic principle beneath the overlay: *People respond to authenticity.* The sturdiest reason for taking supervision from a monk is a respect for his monkishness—a quality that lessens to the same degree that he fancies himself a shop foreman. And the only reason for listening to a teacher is that he or she is just that, a teacher, not the bureaucrat of some buzzer-ringing Kremlin, not the gargoyle posted by the bathroom door.

And so I give my students to understand that I am willing to devote a good deal of time and effort to their learning, but they must be committed to seeing that I have as few distractions from it as possible. An interesting thing happens. When I do indeed turn all my efforts to taking care of my students, they in turn take care of me—as parishioners do their parson, as the workers did their overseer-monk. My students don't ask me the day's date; I ask them, and I make it a point not to know it until they tell me. They tell me much else besides: when I have faculty meetings, when I've forgotten to collect an assignment, when a student from another class needs help, when they plan to be absent for a day or two, then again when they have been absent for a day or two, when my face has turned blue from duplicator ink, when there's something good in the home economics room to eat in place of the lunch I missed to tutor one of them.

Of course this approach will not work without a number of fine students, and I am fortunate to have more than the requisite number. The approach also needs to be sincere and militant. There's a difference between a zealot and a prima donna; students will respect the former even if they find her tiresome, but they will see through the latter very quickly. The teacher who refuses to handle certain "nonsense" because his crossword puzzle is more fun is soon handling nonsense plus bedlam. The same end awaits the teacher who refuses to handle *students'* nonsense but is slavishly ready to handle everyone else's. I let my students see that I am no less angered by the intercom's impertinence than by theirs. I am no less ready to tutor a member of my study hall in geometry—assuming the problem is within my grasp—than I am to read over one of "my" students' essays. If it has to do with learning, I'm for it; if it's anything else, I want it dead.

One hopes that zeal and single-mindedness will give a teacher some authority. However it comes, authority is indispensable. Without authority, a teacher relinquishes the pastoral metaphor and begins "busting heads." In other words, he is reduced to using power. There's a slogan going around on buttons and bumper stickers that reads: Question Authority. It's a fine slogan. But my slogan for teaching reads: Acquire Authority. Question Power.

Teaching on the basis of authority means that one is heeded because one knows something important and because one is entirely confident in that knowledge, its importance, and one's duty to teach it. Teaching on the basis of power means that one is heeded because one has a gradebook, a tough vice principal, a good set of vocal cords, and a list of parents' phone numbers. I doubt any teacher works entirely on authority; a few would seem to be functioning entirely on power. I have no doubt, however, that an "authoritarian" teacher is preferable to a powerful one.

It took me a while to see that, and to see that the arsenal of a teacher's power includes not only gradebooks and detentions but also an adult's wit and intelligence. Like many other younger and idealistic teachers I "questioned authority," my authority, when I ought to have questioned the power of my own mind and the fairness of using it against teenagers. It is one of the ironies of teaching that we are in the greatest danger of using our mental and verbal powers unfairly when we have the greatest desire to treat our students with fairness. We don't want their submission, we say; we want cooperation based on understanding. We don't want to be obeyed because we're the authority figure; we want to be obeyed because we're right. "I'm not into scepters," say we—taking up a club. Blinded by delusions of our own liberality, we actually come close to imitating O'Brien in *1984;* he does not want Winston's submission, but his conversion. And he will spare no amount of patience—and no exercise of his power—to obtain it. Sometimes I think we allow more dignity by demanding compliance than by seeking understanding.

What I count as one of the major blunders of my teaching career occurred when I tried to help a student understand my position. The class was working on a mock SAT test at the conclusion of a short pass/fail course designed to improve test-taking skills. A "pass" grade came as part of a good-faith agreement to take this test and the other exercises seriously. One recalcitrant girl, who had for several weeks been exploiting my all-too-obvious desire to win her by kindness, closed her test booklet long before anyone else had finished. She had simply checked answers off at random and gone to work beautifying her notebook cover. I went to her, asked if she was done—"yes"—if she'd had any problems—"Not really"—if she thought that a review of her answers might be in order—"No." Now my reason for doubting that she'd made a good try was simple enough. There were students in the class a good deal more intelligent than she who were only half through. That was a sensible observation, and a good reason for my making an authoritative demand that she take the test more seriously, or at least an authoritative pronouncement that she had failed to do so. But instead I tried to make my reason *her* reason. "Sue, can you understand why I'm skeptical? If you are legitimately finished," I whispered, "it means you're smarter than everybody else in this class."

That she was not was no news to her or to me, but I'd come very close to saying she was stupid. Perhaps the combination of her curt answers, her pout, and my own disgust with myself for having been too accommodating with her in the past gave me an unconscious desire to hurt. I don't know. She stormed out of the room, and the result of all my efforts to "win" her—including a written apology after this incident—only lost her to me forever. At first she accepted reconciliation, but not for long. I passed her unconditionally, I said in the letter, but requested that she retake the test with me as tutor so that the course would have some purpose for her. She neither came for the test nor spoke to me once the grades went through. Maybe she was one of those people who feel most secure in the role of martyr—but that's not the point. The point is that I, not she, had written the script that made the martyr's role plausible. And I had written it not by believing in my own authority—would that I had done so from the start. I wrote it by trying to be understood.

I'm not saying that I think it's wrong to explain ourselves to students. I am willing to explain anything I do in a classroom, and I think it's good for students to sharpen their critical skills by asking for explanations and by questioning those we give them. But though I explain, I try to discipline myself not to debate. I cannot compel students to "believe" in the purpose or the format of what I teach. I can only hope to inspire belief by the authority of my own conviction.

One of the things a parson-teacher believes in is miracles. That's not to say he works miracles; that has never been his primary role anyway. He is the one who interprets and confirms the miraculous. And miracles are occurring constantly in schools. Kids undergo transformations that make the metamorphoses in Ovid or the plagues in Exodus look mundane. The trouble is that kids often don't believe in their own miracles. They walk on water for a distance, but then, beholding the strong wind and the tumult of the waves, they sink. They need someone who does not entirely believe in liquidity, specific gravity, or untouchability. They need someone who believes that the kingdom of heaven—or whatever we want to call its educational analogue—is at hand.

Once I reprimanded a boy in study hall only to have him say, "Kiss my ass." This is the most intimate proposition a student ever made me, and when I'm an old man I'll probably still be thinking up witty rejoinders. As it was, I responded clumsily, with a suggestion of power, a corresponding loss of authority, and no sense of humor at all. Actually, I was taken completely off my guard. I had never, nor have I since, had a student speak that way to me. And the boy, whom I clearly recognized only after his cheeky remark, had been very polite since coming into my study hall a week earlier. I reined myself in and said I would speak with him after class.

When I did, he told me, almost in tears, who he was. I could "ask around" for verification. He was the boy who'd been thrown out of grammar school for hitting a teacher— something that rarely happens where I teach. It may sound as though he was telling me how lucky I was to have escaped violence or how unlucky I'd be if I ever crossed him again, but I heard no threat. I clasped his hand and listened to the rest of his story. In effect, what he was telling me was that it was best to send him to the office and stay clear of him because he was incurable, untouchable, lost. He may have seemed to be walking on the water of politeness for a week or so, but he was only treading on thin ice. The so-called miracle could be explained. In fact, there was no miracle at all.

His story was new only in its details. I had heard others with the same theme. Don't waste your time on a leper, they had said. One of the bus drivers for our district told me about a girl—"only a little bit of a thing, you know"—who walked onto his bus the first day of school and said to his kneecaps, "You're going to have a big problem with me." "Why's that?" said the driver, wondering how big a problem could come from such a little peanut. "Oh," she said, "there ain't nobody can do nothin' with me." This wasn't a boast or a warning so much as an introduction. That's who I am—the little girl nobody can ever do nothing with. At the high school we had a young man who'd come from a small elementary school, the "poor relation" among schools in our district, who excused himself as the little girl had introduced herself, by disclaiming all possibility of miracles. Whether he flunked or fell or used foul language, his comment was the same: "Don't blame me. I gradyeated Brownin'ton." One of the impending miracles in our school district at this time will be the result of a woman who arrived at that same school with an unshakable belief in the miraculous and a teaching style that looks like a steel tower in a lightning storm. In spirit Mrs. Wasklewicz has said, "Future gradyeates of Brownin'ton, take up your beds and walk!"

To the boy in my study hall I tried to say that taking up your bed and walking doesn't mean you can't trip over your bed. I, too, had stumbled a little in handling his misbehavior. I still believed in his miracle. And there were others in that school, those who'd helped work the miracle to begin with, who also believed it. We went for sodas at the Candlepin restaurant and later to visit his grandfather's farm, and after that the only problem he gave me was threatening to pound a kid who failed to jump at my command. From what I read of the court reports in the local paper, this young man is still falling over his bed. But I continue to believe that he has the ability to carry it; perhaps one day, to cast it away altogether.

Above all else, being a parson means that one tries to be accessible, that one is always in a place where he can be found, and always on the lookout for those who are lost. It means that without the slightest pretensions of being either a doctor or a psychologist, one takes an interest in the physical and emotional health of his pupils. And it means that one makes the rounds of the parish, that he says "Good morning" to people he does not know, that he tells people who cannot see it for themselves that they are "looking good," that he asks about the hunting and the haying, and that he learns enough about both to ask intelligent questions. To be sure, he will observe the difference between "making the rounds" and hanging around; he will pray or at least vow to escape the hell that yawns wide whenever a high school teacher begins to turn into a high school kid. The teacher who tries to impress his students by being "cool," who says, "All this boring crap we teach is worthless anyway, and you know it"—this is the hireling, whose own the sheep are not, who when he sees the wolf coming gets a realtor's license. The true parson will always remember that he is in the world of adolescence but not of it.

That position is one of the glories of the parson's profession. A priest, minister, or rabbi is a man or woman "set apart" from the secular world, yet still a part of it, and from that vantage point he or she is able to love people with a mixture of appreciation, pity, and perhaps a little envy. The celibate priest may pity the man who struggles to support his children, or envy the pleasure that made them. The ordained mother of a congregation may admire *and pity* the laywoman who cannot avoid sexual harassment or dishonest repair bills simply by sporting a clerical collar in public. And both may come to appreciate profoundly the lives of ordinary men and women who try to do what's right, but who are by and large too busy and mortal to spend much time debating the finer points of theology or attending to the latest ecclesiastical fads.

So it is with a teacher, who has been set apart from young people by age and by profession, and yet is in full view of them, and thus able to witness their struggles and admire their graces with an appreciation that peers and even parents may lack. Sometimes I drive behind a school bus, and through its frosted back window I see a few of my kids doing their soundless Punch and Judy show. One of them waves. I wave back, smiling. There's that lovely sense of benediction upon the riot one no longer has in oneself and will scarcely control in those younger. There's that poignant sense of justice in blessing the Carnival because the Lents of school and life can be so hard.

I will always remember walking up the school stairs on the day a hurricane was preparing to work its way up the Connecticut River Valley with a predicted force that had people recalling "the one in '38," which knocked down enough timber to fill every river and lake in the Northeast. The principal came on the intercom to announce that the governor had just declared a state of emergency. All activities were canceled. The buses would arrive in ten minutes. I immediately threw myself flat against the wall just as rivers of joyful students rushed from the classrooms and joined an irresistible human wave washing down the corridor. Adult that I was, I had been trying in vain to reach my insurance company all day. But from one of these kids streaming by I heard the voice of a younger heart, and blessed it. "I'm goin' home to watch the cows fly!"

When I walk or drive through one of these villages on a summer night, and see the girls sitting on a bridge railing, swinging bare legs and waving to the traffic, and the boys leaning against a pickup truck fender with chins high and arms folded (there's a way of pressing the hand up close under the arm so the bicep looks bigger), I think how sweet it must be to feel the night air on your young skin, to watch a lit butt end moving in the darkness like an iridescent conductor's wand as some bull-throwing troubadour re-creates the day he told the teacher "just where to put it," and somebody's eyeful of your own flesh winks and the whole sky fills with northern lights. I'm glad to look at them and think that in moments like these they don't care very much about Shakespeare. That doesn't make Shakespeare or teaching Shakespeare any less important. It simply means that one teaches the plays with humility, knowing that Shakespeare may be no more to some kid than a guy who said some words that add some resonance to a summer night. If that's all, it is enough. It is even more than enough.

By the time a teacher begins putting Shakespeare in perspective, he is well past needing to do the same for his own tentative analogies. Mine come of wearing a certain "hat" on Sundays, and I have reached the point in this discussion where I must either take off the hat or begin talking through it.

Only before closing I would note that there have been a few occasions, both curious and disconcerting, when the parson metaphor became as vivid as the teaching it helped define—when I found it difficult to tell which job was the figurative expression of which.

Several weeks ago I got a call from a student living out in Westmore, at the geographical midpoint between the high school and my parish in Island Pond. Once he had mentioned to me, "My neighbor says you're her minister," and in the setting of the high school, where even the majority of my colleagues were as yet unaware of my other job, his statement first struck me as a case of mistaken identity. After a moment

I said that I was, emphasizing the "lay" adjective almost to the extent of saying that I wasn't.

It was July when the phone rang, and I said I was glad to hear his voice again. I asked about the haying and the fishing. I told him he was "looking good" for college applications next year. I made my figurative benediction upon his seventeen-year-old life. None of this was what he'd called for.

His friend's father had just killed himself.

"I want to know if you would say a prayer for Rodney's dad," he said.

I would, and I did.

Souls in Prison

While there is a lower class I am in it.
While there is a criminal element I am of it;
While there is a soul in prison, I am not free.

—Eugene Debs

*I*n the village of Orleans is a concrete bridge under which the Barton River flows after passing behind the Ethan Allen Furniture mill. On warmer mornings the kids wait there for the bus instead of huddling in the doorways of the Howard Bank and the Kipp Insurance Agency. Afternoons and evenings the older kids return and lean against it, smoking and talking with some of our former students, young men back from the Guard or some work-seeking trip east or south, young mothers holding their first babies and rounding with the next. Now and then I see a sinister-looking man there as well. I am not sure why he is hanging out with people so much younger than himself, but I suspect his reason has more to do with business than with pleasure.

This evening I see my former student Steven. He still wears his hair to his shoulders, which have filled out more since I taught him. He is shirtless, his jeans ride low. He holds out his hand to me, clasps mine in the anachronistic "power to the people" handshake, and squinting through his smoke asks how I am, how my family is doing. He sincerely wants to know. I was an "all right" teacher: I was decent to him, I once gave him sanctuary in my apartment, allowing him to take his final exam there instead of at school, when two muscular farm boys had decided that the world would be a lovelier place with Steven gone from it. He was one of the "druggies" then, and so he remains. He is obviously stoned when I talk to him.

He tells me he's heading out for Stowe after the weekend; he thinks he may have found a construction job. In what comes out something like a joke, but is meant in earnest, I tell him to be careful. "It's easy to get in trouble down there," I say. "Lots of drugs."

"Yeah, man, I know." I bet he does.

Several weeks later I am at a workshop on drug and alcohol education. While the instructor explains how we are going to integrate "substance abuse awareness" into every academic offering in the curriculum—at the same time, of course, as we meet new standards, increase competencies, and learn how to fly—I find my thoughts wandering in a reverie to the bridge. Once again I stand before it in the twilight. I tell the people there that I am sick with watching them waste their lives. I tell them that drug dependence is unhealthy for them and for their society. I tell them that getting high is a pathetic substitute for the valor of living fruitfully and according to a code—all things I believe strongly and tell my students incessantly. Finally, in a desperate personal appeal, I tell them that if they'll give up drugs I won't have to go to substance abuse workshops anymore.

A miracle occurs. They listen to me. Joints and pills drop into the river as tokens of a fresh start. I weep with elation. Then one of the young men turns to me.

"We have done it, Mr. Keizer. Now help us live the productive, meaningful lives you told us about. We are ready. Where do we go from here?"

Where indeed? To the unemployment office to read the

fiche that changes as slowly as the seasons? Back to the farms that are failing every day?

Downstream and out of town, in a trailer by the side of a marsh, lives my student Patty, her mother, and two younger sisters. If the face of the Virgin Mary had been any more innocent, any more fit to belong to the mother of a god than this young girl's face, then I could not have beheld it and lived. As it is, no angel has come to tell Patty she is pregnant; no one is calling the fruit of her womb blessed. I drop by on my way to a fishing hole with the Snugli baby carrier that my daughter has outgrown; it's only in our way now. Perhaps Patty will find it as useful as we did.

Patty takes my leftover as if it were gold and frankincense. "Thanks a real lot, Mr. Keizer." People sometimes talk as though it is the insolence of students that makes teachers despair. I say it is just as often their gratitude, their outrageous gratitude for the trifles we give them.

"Oh, but you give them more than trifles when you teach them. You give them the means to transcend the squalor; you open up the world of the mind. What does Milton say? 'The mind is its own place, and in itself / Can make a heav'n of hell.' " I agree with Dr. Johnson, who pointed out that Milton had put those words in the mouth of Satan: "It is the boast of a devil that has learned to lie." And so are most of the rationalizations for the failure and disaffection of my students.

Not long ago a man came to address my school at a special assembly. I forget whether his talk had a title; I will call it "Steven and Patty." He gave the students some frightening statistics about the extent and the results of early experimentation with sex and drugs. Much of what he said, especially by way of warning, made sense to me—though I could have done with a less doctrinaire tone. When he proceeded to "analyze" the effects of teenage drug use and pregnancy, he offered a curious personal example. "I work two days out of every week," he said, "to pay for the people who've failed to make it in life."

If other teachers are like me, they look back with relief on those incidents where they managed to control their tempers—those times when they took a deep breath, counted to ten, and vowed to visit the employment office on "the next free afternoon." But when I look back on that assembly, and on that man who paid for his good suits and his new cars and his horse farm in Massachusetts and his six charming children to go to the best schools in the country—all from money earned in part by telling the sons and daughters of underpaid mill workers and bankrupt farmers that he works two days a week to "pay for the people who've failed to make it in life," I curse my self-control. I said nothing. I didn't even bother to ask if his two days of lost pay were computed before or after deductions, or if he counted McDonnell Douglas, Chrysler, and the Contras among those who've "failed to make it in life."

I'm tired of seeing people like Steven and Patty end up with crumbs, and of hearing people like this man give the facile reasons why. They explain the crumbs as the result of unwise choices; they fail to recognize how often unwise choices are the result of a crummy life. I'm tired of hearing how our students are not prepared for the "real world" as conceived by those who enjoy the lion's share of its benefits. I say that world needs to be better prepared for them.

We in education talk all the time about how we "care about kids." We speak with the maudlin fraternity of drunks about how much we "care about kids." But care that does not seek to be effectual is dishonest and cheap. I am convinced that we cannot care about kids without caring about the economic, social, and political world from which they come and to which they go.

Those both inside and outside the educational professions

who have taken up the battle cry of educational excellence need to realize that I can give my student the most challenging assignment imaginable—and I try to do just that—but as long as his father needs him to keep the farm from going bankrupt that assignment is not going to be done. Sympathetic politicians and my teachers' union can promise me enough salary to keep a Mercedes-Benz, but what does that do for educational excellence if my student doesn't own a dictionary? We can print our commitment to equality of educational opportunity on every scrap of stationery that comes out of the superintendent's office, but what does it mean when the girls in my class are destined from the start to earn about half of what my boys will earn, when a few of my students will get Apples for Christmas while the rest bring an apple for lunch?

I guess that sentiments such as these run counter to the "current research." Twice now I have attended training sessions and heard, "Twenty years ago we believed that social and economic factors figured heavily in classroom effectiveness. Now we're finding that this is not so." What a pleasant finding! Were the people who did educational research twenty years ago such cretins, or are those doing it now such cretins, or is educational science such a bastion of cretinism that we should make so radical a reappraisal of so fundamental an idea? Or are we conveniently adjusting our research to fit prevailing ideologies? Have we decided that "background" hasn't much to do with educational success at the same time as we have decided that we won't much care even if it does?

Unfortunately, I don't count very much on the members of my profession to resist a trend that accompanies a willingness to pay them more money. If "classroom effectiveness" can be "proven" to have more to do with teachers' salaries than with the incomes of poor single mothers, we're not going to kick too hard at the proofs. Unfortunately, the militancy

of teachers usually comes in two limited forms: the promotion
of ourselves and the influencing of our students. We might
do well to look briefly at each.

"If teachers hadn't promoted themselves, no one else would
have." That is the truth. Most of the gains we teachers have
made have come from our forming unions. I can point to a
number of benefits that I and my family enjoy thanks to the
efforts of organized fellow teachers. I consider myself a grateful if not always a very forthcoming member of the National
Education Association. Some teachers, it is true, are embar-
rassed by unionization. "Professional" types like ourselves
shouldn't have to walk on picket lines or even raise our voices.
I could enjoy doing both. The role of proletarian hero does
not offend my sense of professional dignity at all. It does
clash with my sense of reality.

For the truth is, that should I be involved in a strike, I
would be striking against the farmers, shopkeepers, mill
workers—yes, and some of the well-heeled people—of northeastern Vermont. That does not make the cause of reasonable
compensation for teachers less right; it does make a stance
of righteousness less steady, and the use of militant rhetoric
a bit absurd. I am not the first to note that there are two
Vermonts: the Vermont of ski lodges, craft boutiques, and
fine restaurants; and the Vermont of rusted trailers, failing
farms, and the endless cough. Teachers who work in the latter
are nevertheless able to move somewhat comfortably in the
former. When I go out to eat, I meet more tourists than
neighbors. If I go to "The Queen City" to shop, I meet more
teachers than anyone else I know.

This past summer my wife and I went to a local sawmill
to buy two sharpened cedar posts. A gaunt, toothless man
hobbled over the mud and bark to find the size we wanted.
He came to a heap of posts and began, literally, to sniff
through them for cedar. At the other end of the shed, a boy,
a former Lake Region student, held a log into the grinding

end of a machine. The wood beat around in the circle of his arms like an alligator in a Hula-Hoop. The noise and dust and heat were smothering. Back in the car I said, "You can see why some of our neighbors begrudge us more money." My wife didn't answer. When I looked at her, she was in tears. "I don't want any more money," she said.

Well, there's no need to get carried away. Teachers need more money. And we have the same right as other workers to demand more money in the name of our labor and our material needs. But when we presume to speak in the name of Education, and on behalf of our Students, we are up to something else. We are either adopting a broader agenda or developing a slicker scheme of promotion. We are probably doing a little of both. Yes, we are asking money for schools as well as for ourselves. And even money for ourselves is not without benefit for our students. But the fact remains that teachers are usually the chief beneficiaries of increased funding for education. We need to ask ourselves if it is honest to speak in terms of social justice if our primary objective is to climb the social ladder.

Recently education groups have begun to call for new state and federal methods of funding so as to increase aid for education and distribute that aid more equitably among rich and poor communities. Governor Kunin has just called for such an approach in Vermont. Her proposal is a good one, as courageous as it is probably ill-fated. But I find myself asking: Why just education and not medicine? Why just teachers and not farmers? I wonder how many teachers, even those who affect the most radical stances, recognize the full implications of our asking to be paid not directly by our "customers" but by society at large, not according to "market value" but according to the good we do for our communities. We're pulling on some stout pillars there. The problem is that we agitate like Robin Hood for better pay and vegetate with Prince John once we get the checks.

I suppose the answer to my questions is that education is the logical if "limited" concern of the educational profession. Our aim is to improve schools, not restructure society. My answer to that answer is that we will never improve schools *unless* we restructure society. And my challenge to my profession, if I were in a position prominent enough to make any challenge, would be to ask if we're going to cry out for our impoverished students like outraged mothers, or be courted by politics and business like a bunch of wallflowers who finally got asked to the prom and who will giggle, and lie, and lie down in any position to keep their chance to go there. My challenge for Vermont in particular, where teachers may well have the strongest labor union and potentially the strongest lobby, would be to ask if we are missing a great opportunity to fight for changes more significant than those of our own lifestyle and our own schools' audiovisual rooms.

When I first moved to the Northeast Kingdom, I was told that on the eve of the annual school meeting, certain back-road characters would load their trucks with angry friends and drive them to the high school to vote down the budget. Though I've seen some formidable challenges to the school budget, I never saw the opponents come by the truckload, nor have I ever determined how anyone could survive riding in the bed of a truck on one of our January nights. Still, the image of those trucks has always fascinated me. In waking dreams, I picture them stopping by the light of one little house after another, with chimneys and tail pipes and the mouths of men and women all puffing smoke. They drive toward the school, but to my surprise, they do not stop there. For just a moment, the floodlights on the school grounds afford me a look at one of the drivers. He is an odd-looking fellow, as odd as a college graduate who joins a union, as dubious as a man in his father's blue-collar shirt, bleached white. In fact, he looks remarkably like a teacher, almost like me. I never find out where the trucks are going. I only know for certain what the riders seem to know for certain, that no one's going anywhere on a night this cold unless all go together.

If I ever get to drive one of those fabled trucks, I believe that I may require proof of age from my passengers. I said above that the second "limited" form of a teacher's militancy is influencing students. Perhaps "militancy" is too strong a word for what I want to say here. But we teachers who see so much amiss in our society often seem to feel as though we have a duty to share what we see with our students. After all, if we teach, then what better way to express our commitment to change than by teaching. I have reservations about that. To be sure, I have no reservations about telling kids some of the facts of political, economic, or social life. Elsewhere in this book I argue for acquainting kids with controversial ideas and for encouraging them to take stands. My reservations have to do with what I see as the halfheartedness and folly of "raising our kids' awareness" of their society without raising our society's awareness of its kids.

Our tenth-graders read *Life in the Iron Mills,* by Rebecca Harding Davis, which tells of the ruin of a proletarian artist named Hugh Wolfe. One time my students wanted to know why Hugh didn't just "pack up and leave" the iron mills. Why did he stay? They couldn't understand that. I tried to explain how difficult it would have been for Hugh to go elsewhere, and how unlikely it was that "elsewhere" would have been any different from the scene of his tragedy. They resisted my explanation with such vigor that I knew I had touched some nerve deeper than literary interest. But what was it? I think it was simply this: by saying Hugh Wolfe could not get out of the iron mills, I was telling some of those kids that they'd never get out either. That was neither my intent nor the truth. I doubt I ever did such an about-face as the afternoon I changed from Clifford Odets into Horatio Alger in the space of ten seconds. What right have we to wake people from a flawed but possible dream when we are doing nothing to create a better reality?

In the village of Orleans lives a man who has become for me the symbol of what it means to be a teacher committed to change. His name is James Hayford, and if the Northeast Kingdom has a poet laureate, it is he. But he also taught high school for a number of years, in history, English, and music. When I first met him, he told me about his work at a school in the mid 1960s, where he had acted as an informal mediator during some student demonstrations and succeeded in coaxing students "back into school." At the time I thought he was probably a very conservative fellow. Later, I was surprised to learn that Hayford had been pressured from one teaching job, discouraged from applying for other jobs, investigated by the FBI, and urged by a Vermont newspaper to "go back to Russia"—all for actively supporting the presidential bid of Progressive Henry Wallace in 1948. Neither the merits of student protests nor those of Mr. Wallace's candidacy are the point here. The point is that Hayford elected to take a teacher's stand in full view of a society he wanted to change rather than striking radical poses in front of a few impressionable young people. I think he chose wisely.

Around the time I was getting to know Mr. Hayford, a girl came to me with the rough draft of an essay and asked me to tell her whatever I saw "that was wrong." The essay was entitled "The Free Enterprise System," and she was writing it for a competition sponsored by the Distributive Education Clubs of America. She hoped the essay would enable her to go to Florida with her club chapter. "Just read it over and tell me whatever you see that's wrong." What a lot of faith was in that essay, the faith of my fathers, a faith I cannot entirely abandon—but a faith I knew was not likely to be fulfilled in this girl. Did I see anything wrong? Did I see anything that could be corrected? Did I see anything that could be changed to make it better? There could be a smoother transition between the third and fourth paragraphs. The statement on freedom could be strengthened by an example. "Opportunity" has two "p's." That's all I saw, I told her.

She did get to visit Florida, something Hugh Wolfe could never have done, and she did see a little more of the world thanks to Uncle Sam. The last I heard, she was working in a mill in the Northeast Kingdom and engaged to marry a man who comes from a home even poorer than hers. Perhaps if I teach here long enough, I shall one day read their daughter's essay on free enterprise in order to point out whatever I see that's wrong. I will tell her no more than I told her mother. But perhaps by that time my fellow teachers and I will have found stronger voices for telling our society what we see that's wrong, and more important, what we see that's precious beyond all conceiving. Our students are telling us every day. They are placing their faith, their yearning, and their pain in our hands, often because they have no better place in which to put them. Where will *we* put them?

The first year I taught, the shiest kid in all my classes came up to my desk and presented me with a picture postcard. "This is our cow," she said. At first I was not sure what she wanted me to do with it. Perhaps she was not quite sure herself. Anyway, the picture was mine to keep. I hung it over my desk at home next to Opie's portrait of Dr. Johnson and El Greco's painting of Christ driving the money changers from the temple. Rosie, the Dutch Belt of Brownington, became a sort of sacred cow. And if I could invest Rosie with some recognizable significance, so that all who saw her would know the privations and the promise of my students, I'd send her to wander the countryside as her cousins do in India, and with the same impunity. I'd send her to block and foul the halls of commerce, academia, and government, and to moo the princes unto repentance.

Dust and Ashes

"I have uttered what I did not understand,
   things too wonderful for me, which I
      did not know . . .
I had heard of thee by the hearing of
   the ear,
   but now my eye sees thee;
therefore I despise myself,
   and repent in dust and ashes."

—Job

Sometimes I tell new classes the Hasidic story of a peasant laboring in his fields late in the afternoon preceding the first evening of Passover. He worked hurriedly because once the sun had set he was prohibited from both work and travel—and he needed to be in his household to keep the holiday. But while he worked, the sun set, and he spent the evening all by himself in the darkened field.

Dawn the next morning, his rabbi came walking, and seeing the peasant he asked where he had been the evening before. The peasant explained his predicament.

"That is most unfortunate," said the rabbi. "But I do hope that you managed to say the appointed prayers."

"Oh, rabbi," sighed the peasant, "that was the worst part of the whole experience. Try as I might, I could not remember any of the prayers."

160

"Then how *did* you spend the holy evening?"

"I recited my alphabet," the peasant answered, "and I trusted God to make the words."

In class the story receives a very untheological interpretation. You may feel in the dark, I tell my students, and you may feel all by yourself, but offer what you have, however elementary, and trust that someone in this room will make sense of it, and find it valuable.

I hope that I have written a thoughtful book about teaching. But thoughtful as it may be, in the end it is but an alphabet I recite in the dark. Readers can note the contradictions between passage and passage—those are nothing compared with the contradictions my students will inevitably note between passage and man. I'm waiting for the day—and it will come soon—when one of my blunders leads one of my kids to think: And this is the guy who *wrote a book* about teaching? What a load of crap it must be! Even if none of them thinks it, I will. We can talk about teaching endlessly, but when we meet the student face to face, when he or she speaks to us like Job's God out of the whirlwind of paper and hurry, then like Job we realize that all our talk until this moment is dust and ashes.

Last fall the students at my school walked out of the building before homeroom and began a spontaneous demonstration to protest the removal of some skylights in the gymnasium roof. A petition to save them had failed to overrule the argument that they allowed a significant loss of heat. The remonstrations of both the principal and vice principal failed to get all but a handful of kids back into the school.

My own reaction to the "civil disobedience" was critical, and a little testy. I was not in the mood for it. For one thing, I could think of a good half-dozen issues more deserving of protest than the removal of gymnasium skylights. For another, I have come to regard most of what passes as demonstration these days as little more than a banal form of recreational therapy. I said as much while I and several colleagues watched from the home economics room windows as two boys stormed the roof.

It is hard for me to describe how loathsome I felt in that instant, when one of the teachers, whose daughter was out in the crowd, turned to look at me with great worry in her eyes. Wasn't this exactly what an English teacher with intellectual pretensions was supposed to do in a situation like this: to sit in a secondhand tweed jacket like a pompous ass on the window ledge and glibly pass judgment on the unsophisticated? In trying to point out the demonstration's banality, I had come face to face with my own.

But what to do? I went down to the principal's office and tried to make suggestions. Cancel classes and have the kids come into the gym for an open forum on the issue. But the administration was convinced that further negotiations were futile, and they were probably right.

I left the office and watched from the corridor windows. One gigantic boy, a "new kid" without much sense, single-handedly pulled a ladder down from the building, trapping the workmen on the roof. Three or four other kids ran forward immediately in order to put it up again, but a workman on the ground, enraged by what had just happened and interpreting the kids' movement as a second assault, rushed at them menacingly and chased them back. I saw the kids' faces— they wore that look kids get when they have meant to do well and are rebuffed. And they were kids from my class, my kids.

But what to do? Where is your educational philosophy when the ladders fall to the ground, and the passing bells ring and nobody comes, and the intercom talks and nobody listens? I went upstairs and out the side door. A small group of tough guys stood on the bank defiantly smoking cigarettes, laughing simultaneously at the demonstration and at the adults' inability to stop it. I walked past them and toward the parking lot where the other kids were marching in a circle. I meant to talk with one of them to find out more of what was going on.

A sophomore girl ran up to me. "Mr. Keizer," she said, "is this dumb? Are we being dumb?" I don't know if a kid has ever asked me a question in more earnest. It was like a magnification of the question "Am I going to flunk?" with an echo of the question "How come on television, when there's somebody from Vermont, they always make him look dumb?"

"No, Carol, you are not dumb . . . I guess I'm not as excited as you about the issue . . . I think some things need to be done differently, I—" Looking up from her face, I discovered myself standing in the center of a throng of students, with others running to the outskirts, where they were hushed by those in front. All those eyes, all those faces turned toward me—what does a teacher do when the kids walk out of class? I decided he tries to hold class outside.

I told them the first thing that had to be realized was that the workmen were not the enemy, and the first thing that had to be done was to be reconciled with them. The kids knew this already. I suggested a peace offering of sodas; the kids went one better with coffee and doughnuts.

I told them that demonstrations die of their own inertia. I told them they needed to organize and to keep the troops creatively active—have them pick up trash off the grounds, sing songs, anything, but not to let them get bored or straggle off into anarchy. I told them to send representatives to the smoking bystanders, who saw this as just a larger-than-usual ruckus, and invite them to join or to get lost. I told them to stamp out with a vengeance any horseplay, anything that might hurt a student or involve the police, who by this time were standing watch. I told them to formulate what they wanted into a few simple words, to elect leaders, and to stay in communication with the main office.

Finally, I told them that they had set themselves a task which required them to be more responsible and better behaved than they had ever had to be in the classroom. The authority figures were gone now—there was no one to say,

"Be good." The kids were only as good as they themselves decided to be, and they would be effective only insofar as they could be good. "There are some people who are no doubt waiting for you to act like jerks so they can put down what you're fighting for. But you are not jerks. You have to show them that."

I turned to walk back into the building. They cheered. I won't say it didn't matter to me. I won't say that I didn't go straight to the principal and tell him what I had done, so there would be no misunderstandings.

An hour or so later I was teaching in my classroom once again. The superintendent had met with the students' elected leaders and agreed to call an emergency meeting of the school board and community if the students agreed to return to classes. In general, the fair-mindedness and restraint with which our administration reacted helped to prevent a trying day from turning into an inglorious one. By afternoon most of us were too occupied with ordinary business to reflect much on what an extraordinary time we had had. That is one of the graces of teaching: it leaves you no leisure in which to gloat or pine.

At three o'clock, with the kids on their way to the buses in their usual elation at having ended the day, and an added elation at having *won* it, a young boy stopped in my doorway—one of those bespectacled, elfin kids whose sudden appearance almost prompts one to exclaim, "Where on earth did *you* come from?"

"Mr. Keizer, thank you for your help today," he said.

"Well, it was you guys who did it. The students carried it off."

"That's true," he said with great solemnity. "But you showed us the way."

I showed them the way. That is all a teacher *can* do— show the way. But how often, even in the very act of showing it to them, are we not groping for it ourselves?